BK   LB   @ Pa

THE MOTHER LODE

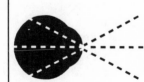

This Large Print Book carries the
Seal of Approval of N.A.V.H.

A MAN OF HONOR NOVEL

THE MOTHER LODE

GARY FRANKLIN

THORNDIKE PRESS
A part of Gale, Cengage Learning

GALE
CENGAGE Learning™

Detroit • New York • San Francisco • New Haven, Conn • Waterville, Maine • London

GALE
CENGAGE Learning·

Copyright © 2007 by Gary McCarthy.
Thorndike Press, a part of Gale, Cengage Learning.

Thorndike Press® Large Print Western.
The text of this Large Print edition is unabridged.
Other aspects of the book may vary from the original edition.
Set in 16 pt. Plantin.
Printed on permanent paper.

LIBRARY OF CONGRESS CATALOGING-IN-PUBLICATION DATA

Franklin, Gary, 1942–
    The mother lode : a man of honor novel / by Gary Franklin.
        p. cm.
    ISBN-13: 978-1-4104-0530-2 (alk. paper)
    ISBN-10: 1-4104-0530-3 (alk. paper)
    1. Large type books. I. Title.
PS3568.O346M68 2008
813'.54—dc22   2007046312

Published in 2008 by arrangement with The Berkley Publishing Group,
a member of Penguin Group (USA) Inc.

Printed in the United States of America
1 2 3 4 5 6 7 12 11 10 09 08

THE MOTHER LODE

1

Joe Moss left California on a tough Spanish mule with only one thought on his mind . . . get over these towering Sierras and find his beloved Fiona and their bastard child somewhere on the Comstock Lode. He had been a mountain man, a Santa Fe mule skinner, and a wagon master, but now he felt as if he'd been nothing but a failure.

Tall and angular, at forty years of age, he'd killed and scalped enough men to warrant a ticket straight to hell, but in sweet Fiona McCarthy and the child they had created, he felt that he might somehow find redemption, if not in the eyes of the Lord, then at least in his own. Only days before, he'd learned that the only woman he'd ever loved had borne his child, which they'd conceived on an ill-fated wagon train four years earlier. As wagon master and chief scout, Joe was responsible for bringing those sixty wagons out from St. Joseph, and he'd done a pretty good job, too. But then he'd fallen in love with Brendan McCarthy's daughter, and lain with Fiona in the grass while one of the stock tenders had gotten his scalp lifted. And for that single hour of joy and pleasure, he'd been sent packing when his train reached Fort Laramie.

"I thought I could drive Fiona out of my heart with liquor and other women," he told the hard-laboring mule as it trudged up toward Donner Pass. "But I never did. I would have let her go and lived a life of regrets, except now I just found out she bore my child. Boy or girl, it don't matter to me. The baby has my blood and is birthed from my seed. Mule, as God is my witness, I mean to give both Fiona and our child my name . . . if that Irish girl will show forgiveness and still have me."

Joe Moss had lived a hard, free life, and it wasn't in his nature to attach to anything . . . especially a woman. To his way of thinking, if you loved something, it was just too damned painful to lose it, so it was better never to love. But he had fallen in love with sweet Fiona, and then brought her nothing but heartache and shame. Maybe if her mother hadn't fevered and died on the trail, and her father hadn't been such a roaring asshole, things would have gone smooth.

8

But when Fiona's mother had passed beside the Platte River, Fiona had sworn to look after her daddy, and so she'd been bound to keep her word. Joe didn't blame Fiona for honoring a deathbed promise to her mother, but it sure had caused them both a dung pile of pain.

"Some men are lucky at cards and some are lucky at finding gold or fortune," Joe told the poor mule as it labored up toward the high pass, "but me . . . well, I've never been lucky at anything, and good only at stayin' alive be it fightin' red man or white."

The mule was really struggling because of the steep grade and high altitude. Joe had bought the little beast in Denver, and it had packed all his gear while he'd almost killed a good Appaloosa gelding on his frantic quest to reach Fiona in California. The Palouse had carried Joe's weight and run its heart near to burstin', and he'd left the horse right about here . . . left it to live . . . or die . . . as it would, and he'd cursed himself for his desperation and cruelty.

Joe Moss reckoned that he had a great big hole in himself where his soul should have rested. And he believed that his only hope for this world or the next rested in making things right with Fiona and taking her as his wife . . . if she'd have him.

But what if Fiona was married? They'd told him in California that her father had married her off once to a prospector in the expectation of having a rich claim on the Feather River. But the claim had proven a bust and Brendan McCarthy had killed the prospector in a rage, and taken his daughter to the Comstock Lode. Maybe that sonofabitch had married Fiona off a second time to another miner, this one a hard-rock man who worked deep under the Comstock Lode.

Just the thought of poor Fiona being married to a man she did not love and bearing a child whose father she thought never again to see was enough to send Joe Moss into utter despair. And what of their child? Had it lived . . . or had it died? If it had died, then he'd fathered a child he'd never known or seen. Gawd! It was enough to make a grown man weep.

"Hurry along, mule!" Joe cried, jumping off the animal when it staggered and seemed ready to drop. "Hurry along!" he urged as he tugged on the lead rope with sweat pouring down his bearded face into his dirty buckskins.

The mule was nearly dead when they reached a sorry little settlement named Pine Town just an hour before sundown. It wasn't much of a place at all, hard-looking and with only a few stores fronting a muddy red rut of road.

"We'll stop here for the night," he told his badly flagging mule. "I'll get you some grain and all the hay you can swallow. Maybe some new shoes because I hear that the Comstock Lode ain't nothin' but a barren mountain with no trees nor grass nor any sweet water. It's just a hell hill of pure gold and silver."

Joe found a livery and dismounted. The owner came out and said, "Looks like you've been doin' some hard travelin', mister."

"We have been," Joe admitted with some shame.

The livery owner was a man in his early sixties, dirty, with bib overalls tucked into the tops of boots worn out at the heels. He wore a little top hat thick with dust and it rested on his bat ears. Beyond him, Joe could see a corral with five horses inside and a barn that seemed to have more air in the walls than wood. Two big Missouri mules saw Joe's little Spanish mule and brayed a challenge at the beaten animal.

"You want I should put your mule in with those two?" the liveryman asked. "Be cheapest for you."

"No, thank you," Joe told the man, knowing that his little mule would get bullied and bitten. "Put him in his own stall with fresh straw and grain him good, then feed him all of your best hay that he can stomach."

The livery owner frowned. "Little skinny fella like that ain't hardly worth botherin' about, mister. Why, he ain't worth much of nothin'."

"I know that," Joe said, feeling irritated by the comment, "but he's all I got and he's given me his best so take good care of him for the night. How much added to let me sleep in your hay and wash in your water trough?"

"Two dollars for you both will handle the charge and I'll loan you a bar of lye soap. You *do* sort of smell rank, mister. Why didn't you jump in a river on your way up from Sacramento?"

" 'Cause I don't swim so good and I don't want to die by drownin'," Joe confessed. "Rivers hereabouts are all fast. Probably drunken prospectors drownin' in 'em most every day."

"They used to do that," the liveryman admitted. "Maybe not every day, but at least every week. Then the gold panned out and they raced over these mountains to the

Comstock Lode. Ain't no rivers over there in Nevada, so I heard. Ain't much of any good water in Nevada . . . just lots of snakes, alkali flats, gold, and even some silver."

"How come you didn't go with 'em when the gold panned out on this side of the Sierras?" Joe asked.

The man scratched his crotch, then poked a finger in one of his big bat ears and screwed it around some before he said, " 'Cause I'm an old fart and I like the green of the pines and the wildflowers in the meadows. They say that there ain't a blade of grass or a wildflower up on the Comstock Lode. Don't sound like the Promised Land to me, stranger. Don't sound like anything but Hell."

"That may be true, but I still got to go there," Joe said, as much to himself as to the liveryman. "I got to get there just as fast as I can do 'er."

"I could tell that by the looks of that mule. You'll kill him if you don't let him rest here a few days. Not that he's worth much in savin'."

Joe thought about that and about what he had done to the poor Appaloosa that had tried so valiantly to deliver him to California only a few weeks earlier when he'd run it west over these very same mountains.

"Mister," he said, "the truth is that I kill most things that I'm around. And one of these days I'll probably kill myself and do the whole damned world a favor."

The liveryman laughed outright. He had a big, booming laugh and it showed that he was missing most of his front teeth. To be right truthful, he had a powerful rank smell on himself and also needed a dunkin' and a bar of soap. But Joe didn't see no point in mentioning that fact.

"You're mighty hard on yourself, stranger. Mighty hard. And unless I judge it wrong, you've been a trapper and Indian trader."

"You judge me good."

The liveryman stepped back and put his hands on his hips. "You're wearing tanned buckskins and we don't see that much anymore. And a bowie knife, which isn't all that unusual. But I ain't seen a man carry a damned tomahawk like that for many a moon."

"Took it off an Indian who didn't want to let 'er go. Want to see my scalps?"

The liveryman's eyes widened in the gloom. "You got real human scalps?"

"I don't scalp no critters for showin' off," Joe said. "And hey, listen, I'll trade you two of my best scalps for the night's food and bedding for me and my mule."

14

The man scratched his round and un-shaven face and his eyes could not hide his excitement. "They be the *real* thing?"

"They be," Joe assured him. "You can have what once belonged to a white man, Mexican, or Indian. Don't matter to me. Every one of 'em came off a man that made the mistake of tryin' to rob or kill me. I never back-shot no man nor killed one that didn't desperately need killin'."

"Well, I believe I surely would like to see some real people scalps. That ain't somethin' you get to see or touch every day."

"Reckon not."

"Did you . . ." The liveryman's question trailed off into silence.

"Did I what?"

"Take 'em *all* by yourself, mister? I mean, every last one of 'em?"

"I did. I take no pride, but also no shame, in that true fact."

"Which weapon did you use?" The liveryman gestured toward Joe's weapons. "Knife, gun, or that big sumbitchin' tomahawk?"

"All three," Joe told him.

"You're a mountain man true enough," the liveryman said with a touch of awe and fear mixed in his voice. "And I will treat you and your mule fairly."

"Best that you do."

Joe leaned his Henry rifle against the barn and went over to his mule to open his pack. He quickly found the leather bag of scalps and began pulling them out one by one.

"Holy shit!" the liveryman said. "Holy hogshit! They *are* real!"

From the man's reaction, Joe Moss could see that he could have easily made a trade with only one of the scalps instead of the promised two. But a deal was a deal and he always stood by his word, it being a matter of personal honor.

"I'll take this one and this," the liveryman told him, hands reaching out with fingers shaking from excitement.

"This long, greasy one belonged to a brave Sioux warrior and I shot him off his pony. This lighter one was a white man that I killed while I was leading my wagon train out of old St. Joe."

"Why'd you kill someone on your wagon train?"

Joe didn't want to speak of it, but knew he must now that he'd made his admission. "The white man raped a girl on my train; then the fool up and stole my damned horse. Even worse, he told everyone that I was layin' down with the unmarried girl I loved and love still. The bastard shamed her, and that caused me to scalp him just before

16

I put a noose around his neck and hauled him off the ground."

The man's fingers touched the scalp, then quickly retracted as if they'd been burned by the deed. "You *strangled* that fella to death instead of givin' him a good drop so that you'd break his neck?" the liveryman asked, now unable to take his eyes off the pale scalp.

"Yep," Joe cheerfully admitted. "The sonofabitch's name was George Tarlton. Wasn't much more than a boy, but old enough to know better and pay for his misdeed."

The old man's liver-spotted hand stretched out a second time to touch Tarlton's long hair. "Why, mister, it's still crusted with his . . . his *blood!*"

"Why, a'course it is! Scalpin' is a bloody business. And I reckon our business is done if you can get me that bar of soap and maybe some gunnysacks to dry with."

"Hell, yes, I will!" the older man said, snatching the two scalps and backing away as if Joe Moss were a dying leper. "Just . . . just tie the mule up and give me a minute. I got some beans on the stove in the back. You hungry?"

"Do bears shit in these tall pines?"

"Yes, they do!" the man cried, hurrying

off with both scalps dangling from his dirty hands. "And I'll feed you beans till you fart like a fat goat!"

Joe grinned and began to unsaddle the little mule. He noted that it had fresh cinch sores that were bleeding. Blood on scalps, blood on the mule, and blood on his soul.

It might be better for Fiona if I just went away like the cold north wind, he thought.

"Joe Moss," he said with a sad shake of his head, "if you were a good man, you'd put a bullet in your brain this very minute. Be a mercy to mankind . . . and maybe to Fiona and your child should it still be alive."

He stood beside his mule with his head down feeling low and ugly and evil because he had hurt most everything he'd ever loved or touched that was good. Was it too late to change and make up for past mistakes and wrongs?

"Here's soap and a towel, mister. You okay?"

Joe snapped out of his dark reverie. "Yep."

"Then hurry 'cause it's getttin' dark. You can use that old horse watering trough out back so no man or woman will see you."

"If they see me, it's on their eyes and it won't matter," Joe said. "But I ain't any more to look at than this poor mule. And I got a sight more scars."

18

"From Indians?"

"Some of 'em."

The liveryman reached way out to hand Joe the lye soap and two grain sacks that were anything but clean. "Mister, I see hard men comin' and goin' every day. Seen 'em all my damned life. But I think you might be the hardest man I ever did lay eyes upon."

Joe nodded in complete agreement. "I expect that may be so," he said. "I should have been killed long ago, but for some reason it's me that does all the killin'."

The liveryman opened his mouth to say something, then changed his mind and backed away with respect. "I'll get you a plate of beans when you're done with the horse water."

"Thank ye."

"And I won't tell anyone who traded me those scalps. I wouldn't want it to come down against you."

"Do as you think best, but it wouldn't be a trouble."

"Meaning that you'd kill anyone who came at you about those scalps? That be your *true* meaning. Right, mister?"

Instead of answering, Joe just stared at the liveryman with his piercing blue eyes and greasy long black hair until the liveryman gulped and backed away fast.

2

Joe awoke before dawn as was his habit, and because he slept in his buckskins, it didn't take much time for him to grope his way outside the barn and then find his mule waiting in the corral. "Did that fella grain you well?" he asked, opening a small sack of oats and allowing the mule to have some extra feed to start his day off right.

The mule inhaled the oats, and then allowed itself to be tied up while Joe refilled the sack so he'd have feed for the animal at the end of another hard day should they be camping out along the Truckee River tonight. After that, Joe crapped in the corral and washed himself in the trough, then saddled and mounted the mule.

"Time to get along," he told the animal as he laid his Henry rifle across his saddle. "Donner Pass is still miles away and I don't much cotton to the idea of spending the night where all those poor unfortunate members of the Donner Party died. I'd like us to get down past Donner Lake on the river."

Joe had been over Donner Pass before and the area, while incredibly beautiful, always gave him the spooks. It had only been fifteen years earlier that the ill-fated wagon train bound for California had gotten a late start and ended up being trapped in the high pass. Of the eighty-nine emigrants who had set out from Fort Bridger, only forty-five had survived the ordeal, and it was rumored that some of them had resorted to cannibalism. Joe didn't know about that, but he had heard that the survivors, who had been thought to have eaten human flesh in a desperate hope to avoid starvation, had been vilified by the Californians. That seemed wrong to Joe Moss, for he knew with certainty that he would eat the flesh of a dead person if that was all that would keep him alive. And he also knew from reading and from the words of Indians that ancient peoples had been sacrificed and eaten as a means of survival.

"I'd sure rather eat a skinny, worn-out dog or a mule than a fellow human," Joe told his mount. "But mostly I prefer elk and buffalo meat to all others. Mutton and beef are what I can get most of the time, but wild

22

game is my natural preference."

As morning light appeared and the sun lifted slowly in the eastern sky, Joe began to meet mule skinners and other travelers coming down from the pass on their way to California.

"Mornin'," he would call to each passing party. "How's the weather in Nevada these days?"

"Fine and dandy!" most would yell back without stopping. "But there's a storm brewin' and it could bring some rain and maybe even snow if we don't get down to the Sacramento Valley soon."

Joe knew that everyone who crossed over through Donner Pass was keenly aware of the terrible fate of the Donner Party and so they were especially nervous about getting trapped by a late snow. Hell, at this altitude, it could snow as late as June, and when that happened, the big freight wagons would mire down in the red mud so deep they would have to be unloaded before being pulled free.

At noon and less than a thousand feet from the summit, Joe saw a strange-looking freight wagon being pulled by a collection of oxen, mules, and horses, all of which were in terrible shape. There were ten animals and not a one of them looked as if it would last another day. Even worse, the two freighters were cracking their whips and cussing like sailors. As Joe drew nearer, he saw that one of the animals was none other than his old Palouse, the horse that he had nearly killed making a run for California.

"Hold up there!" Joe called, raising his hand as he approached the wagon, which showed no sign that it was going to do anything but run him over if he did not yield and leave the road. "I said hold up!"

The man holding the lines was huge and bearded, thicker than Joe, but probably not any taller. It was the other man that was doing the mean bullwhip work and had the backs of the struggling team bloody, causing Joe to grit his teeth in anger.

"Hold up, damn you!" Joe snapped, not reining off the road, but instead raising his Henry rifle and pointing it directly at the driver.

"Get out of the way, you sonofabitch!" the man with the lines bellowed. "We got heavy lumber on this wagon and we ain't stoppin' for nobody!"

Joe quickly reined up the little mule, now growing very nervous about the onrushing team and wagon. He put the stock of his big rifle to his shoulder and in one smooth motion took aim and fired. The heavy boom of the weapon filled the high corridor of pines along the road, and the driver's hat went flying from his head to reveal that he was completely bald.

"Sonofabitch!" the one with the bloody bullwhip screamed, dropping his whip and reaching for the pistol strapped to his side.

Joe levered in another shell and took aim on the smaller man while shouting, "If you draw iron, mister, then you're as good as dead right *now!*"

The driver hauled up on his reins and applied the wagon's brake. It screeched in protest and smoked, but the wagon came to a stop just a few feet from Joe Moss and his now nervously dancing Mexican mule.

"Are you crazy!" the driver screamed, fumbling around with big fingers atop his head where his hat was supposed to ride. "Are you plumb loco!"

"Nope," Joe said, watching the bullwhip man. "And I mean what I said about either of you drawing iron against me. I hit what I shoot at pretty near every time and my next two bullets are gonna splatter your brains."

"What the hell do you want? Is this a damned holdup?" the smaller man demanded. " 'Cause if it is, you're shit out of luck, mister. We ain't carryin' no cash. Just a load of lumber from Truckee bound for a

25

settlement down on the American River."

Joe lowered the barrel of his rifle. "I got no room to brag on being kind to animals, but you men are the worst sonofabitches on stock that I've ever seen and I've seen a lot. What the hell are you skinnin' their backs for with that whip and why haven't you fed that team right?"

"Who are you?" the driver snarled. "A damned crazy animal lover? No, you can't be because that sorry mule you're riding looks like it ain't been treated all that well, either."

"More to my shame," Joe admitted. "But you don't see me whipping him bloody."

"What do you want?" the smaller of the pair challenged, picking up his bullwhip and coiling it in his strong hands. "Or did you just damn near shoot Edgar's head off for the fun of it?"

Joe lowered his rifle a trifle and replied, "It's about that Palouse horse you're killin'."

"You mean the spotted Appaloosa?"

"That's the one," Joe said. "He's mine."

"The hell you say!" the driver shouted. "We bought him from a miner! Paid him five dollars and that was too damn much. He's weak and is about to die."

"Last week I left him on this trail not five

miles from where we are right now," Joe explained. "I thought he was dead because I'd run him too far and too hard. But now it fills my heart with some gladness to see that he lived. And I want to buy him from you today."

The two freighters exchanged glances reflecting amazement. Then, the driver turned to Joe and said, "You are battier than a bedbug, mister. And if you hadn't gotten the drop on us, we'd have run you down and it would have been good riddance to the world."

"That's probably the first true thing I've heard come out of your mouth," Joe agreed. "But it don't change the fact that I feel that I owe that Palouse horse a second chance and I had grown to admire the animal when it was fit and strong. That's why I need to buy him back."

"Well, I'm tellin' you that he ain't for damned sale!" the man with the bullwhip screamed. "And you're wastin' our time!"

"How much?" Joe said, deciding to ignore the outburst. "State your price."

"Only a hundred dollars," the driver said, the corner of his mouth turning into a grin of contempt. "You want him, then that's what it'll cost you."

"You're getting' five," Joe said. "You told

27

me that's what you paid for him and it was too much."

"Go to hell! It ain't worth our time to unhitch him for that little amount of money, and besides that, we need him in the team."

"It's all downhill for you boys from here on to Sacramento," Joe reminded them. "But just to show that my heart is in the right place, I'm going to give you *ten* dollars. That way you double your money and have got hard use out of the Palouse in the bargain."

The driver's smile died. "You got ten dollars in gold coin?"

"I do."

"You probably got more than that, I'd guess."

Joe pulled out his bag of gold coins and currency and selected a gold eagle. "Don't suppose you'd rather have a fine scalp to show off to your friends?" he asked hopefully.

The two men, looking down from the advantage of their high wagon perch, saw that Joe's sack was heavy with coins and cash, and something very deadly passed between them.

The man with the bullwhip shot his arm forward and the long, wicked whip sailed expertly over the beaten team and struck

Joe's little mule between the eyes. The mule bolted in pain and fear, sending Joe and his wealth spilling to the ground. Then the driver made a grab for a shotgun placed between his feet. Joe saw the shotgun come up even as he rolled off the mule, came to his feet, and grabbed the tomahawk at his belt.

The driver would have killed him for certain, but the shotgun got tangled in the ends of his heavy reins and he couldn't get it quickly free and clear. Joe had no such of a problem, and he threw the tomahawk so that it sailed end over end in a silver blur until its sharp blade buried deep in the driver's chest.

Fortunately, the bullwhip man wasn't a quick thinker, or he might have either surrendered or used the gun on his hip. Instead, the fool tried to use his bullwhip a second time against Joe. But the whip was only leather, while Joe's bowie knife was made of the finest steel. He slashed at the bullwhip and cut it off short, then threw the knife aiming for the heart, but missing a little and hitting the throat.

"Eeegghhh!" the smaller man gagged, blood gushing like a fountain from his severed carotid artery.

"Easy, mule." Joe calmed his little mule

and dismounted while the frightened team struggled to drag the freight wagon against the force of its set brake. The mule had a deep nick in its forehead and was bleeding, but at least it had not lost an eye to the bull-whip.

"Whoa up there," he said. The freight wagon skidded a foot or two, and then Joe was reaching for the Palouse, calming it down and rubbing its cheek like he had done in the past.

The freighters were both dead, and Joe pulled them off their perches and then dragged them deep into the forest. They were carrying about fifty dollars between them, and that was a nice bonus. Joe pocketed their money and collected their weapons, which he could resell on the Comstock.

"Ain't got time to properly bury you fools," Joe explained. "But I want you to know that I've enjoyed doin' business with the both of you. Sorry it ended up so bad, but it was *your* fault, not mine."

Joe kicked pine needles over their bodies until they were well covered. He started to leave, and then said, "Oh, boys. I want you to know that I'll take a lot better care of your poor team than you did. But I think I'll turn 'em around and over another pass and down into the Carson Valley. I don't want to run into any of your friends and have to kill 'em too."

Joe didn't look back at the two piles of pine needles. He regretted having to skewer that pair, but they'd needed killing and it was brought on by their own foolishness, not his. And after all, he had offered them a five-dollar profit in good faith.

After that, what else could a fighting man be expected to do?

3

When Joe reached Donner Pass, he expertly turned the freight wagon loaded with prime lumber down a little-used southern road that eventually brought him to the western shore of Lake Tahoe. There was considerable traffic along the lakeshore, but he was certain that the wagon and its mixed team had not traveled this road before and would not be recognized.

He rested the team that night beside the lake where there was a lush meadow, and he cut ropes to make them all hobbles so that they could graze to their heart's delight.

Joe shot two squirrels and skinned, gutted, then roasted them over a little campfire. The stars were so bright overhead, you felt as if you could reach out and tickle their bellies. Up this high, the night sky was amazingly bright, and there were boats out on the lake dragging logs along the moonlit lake's vast surface to sawmills.

Joe wandered over to the Palouse horse and spent a half hour just rubbing its head, neck, and shoulders. "You know," he told the half-starved and badly abused animal, "I have done many things that I've been ashamed of and most I could not take back. But finding and marrying Fiona and giving our child my name is something I can do right. And helping you get back to your old powerful self is another that I aim to do as a way of righting a wrong. I'll sell the mule and the others in the team when we get down into the Carson Valley. I won't get much for 'em, but they cost me nothing so that is okay. But you, spotted horse, I'm going to hang onto and you'll carry me up to the Comstock Lode. Once there, I'll find and marry Fiona and I'll make sure you never again suffer abuse. How is that for fair and square?"

As if the big gelding understood, it nodded its head and then went back to devouring the sweet alpine meadow grass. Joe returned to his campfire and finished off the squirrel meat, then picked his teeth with the bowie that had killed a man earlier that day.

He'd carried about seven hundred dollars before he'd met the freight wagon that had instantly made him a relatively prosperous man. Because with the wagon filled with sawn pine boards fit for immediate use in building, Joe figured he was now worth a thousand dollars . . . easy. Maybe twelve hundred if he got much of anything at all for his mule and the team.

Twelve hundred dollars was more money than he'd ever had in his lifetime. Why, the most he'd made trappin' beaver in a season was only about six hundred. Still, he reckoned that prices would be expensive on the Comstock Lode. They always were in the roaring gold camps.

Joe wondered if Fiona would want to stay up in Virginia City after they were married. She might, but he hoped not. Joe had never been up on barren Sun Mountain where the mines were all deep and hard rock and there was little wood or water. And he wasn't exactly excited about going there now, much less remaining if that should be Fiona's wish. But by gawd, this mountain man would become a miner or whatever else that woman wanted him to be.

"I'm no spring chicken anymore," he said to the fire. "But I'm still more man than most and I can outwork, outfight, and outdrink most any fella."

Joe ran his fingers through his long, tangled hair and then his full, bushy beard,

34

which was greasy and unkempt. In the firelight, he studied his soiled and worn-out buckskins and knew that he was a wild and undesirable-looking specimen of manhood.

"I will get a haircut and shave before I call upon Fiona," he vowed to the flames. "And I'll buy myself a whole set of new clothes . . . a fine hat and a new pair of boots . . . if I can stand to wear 'em instead of these comfortable old moccasins. That way, when Fiona sees me after so many years apart, she will not think me unclean and unfit for marriage."

Joe lit his pipe with a twig from the fire and inhaled the raw tobacco he'd bought in California. He'd smoked better, and he wished he had some whiskey to drink as he lay under these beautiful stars. But he didn't feel for a serious lack of anything, really. He was close to Fiona and his child now . . . he could almost feel their presence less than a hundred miles to the east.

"I'm a'comin'," he whispered up at the stars while wondering if Fiona might also be looking at these very same celestial bodies. If so, maybe their souls would connect right now and she would know that he was so very near and hear his fervent promise.

"I'm a'comin', my love," he vowed. "Ain't nothin' can stop me."

Joe fell asleep sometime around midnight, and when he awoke in the morning, the air was so cold and clean to his lungs that he snorted like a colt and felt just as frisky.

The team of mules and horses, however, didn't look much better for their night of grazing and resting. Joe knew that once livestock were far down on their natural weight, it took weeks or even months to fatten them. These animals had been long abused and overworked, and it would take quite some time for them to fully recover.

Joe hitched the sorry-looking team to his new freight wagon, not caring that he was getting a late start. He followed the wagon road south along the edge of Lake Tahoe, admiring the view every step of the way. This lake, more than any other he'd seen, was deep, deep blue. So blue and clear that you could see big rocks fifty or maybe even a hundred feet under the surface. Oh, Lord, but it was cold, clear water. So cold that it made your bones ache just to put your feet into it.

"It'll be warmer down in the Carson Valley," he told the team with their cut and scabby backs laid waste by the bullwhip, which he had thrown into the brush. "And down in the valley the grass will be tall and green and you'll get fat and handsome . . .

every last one of you. Even you, mule!" he called over his shoulder to the faithful beast that he'd tied to the tailgate.

Joe grinned up at the sun and felt very good. When he came upon a traveler, he said, "How far is the pass down to the valley?"

"Which one?"

"Ain't there a road down to Carson City not far away?"

"There is but it ain't hardly fit for travel. Real steep and rutty. If I was you and had as poor a team as the one that you're driving, I'd go just a ways farther and take the road leading down into the little town of Genoa."

"Where is that?" Joe asked.

"It's only twenty miles or so south of Carson City. It's a Mormon community and they say it's the first settlement in Nevada. Them Mormons are clannish, but they sure know how to cook a meal for a travelin' man. They'll feed up those animals, too. Like I said, they're clannish as clams, but always deal with outsiders fair and square. They are hardworking and honorable people."

"Are they miners?" Joe asked.

"Hell, no," the man said with a friendly smile. "All farmers. They got some good farming and grazing land down around Genoa. You go there and you'll see what I mean."

"I wouldn't mind selling this wagon, team, and the lumber to those Mormons."

"They'll buy it . . . if your price is fair."

"It'll be fair, all right," Joe vowed. He liked the idea of selling everything to a small town off the beaten path where no one was likely to recognize the wagon or livestock. "How far to the road that will take me down to Genoa?"

"Only about eight miles, maybe ten from here. But do you want some good advice?"

Joe grinned. "Sure, so long as it's free."

"I'd camp at the head of the road tonight and hit the grade down into Genoa come daybreak. It's a better road than the one down to Carson City, but it's still mighty steep with plenty of sharp switchbacks. You got a good brake on that wagon?"

Joe laid his hand on the brake, not sure how to answer. "It seems to work tolerable."

"It had better be *more* than tolerable or that wagon, being so heavy with lumber, might get to rollin' too fast and send you and everything else over the side. You'd best take 'er real slow and careful, mister."

"Thank you for your good advice," Joe told the man with genuine appreciation. "I certainly will take it to heart."

Joe continued on until he came to the road leading off the mountain down to Genoa. A posted sign warned that the road was steep and about ten miles long with pullouts where wagons could pass coming up or down. The sign warned freighters never to take the road when it was covered with snow or ice.

"Ain't no snow or ice to worry about now," Joe said as he drove the team onto a meadow and prepared to camp for the night. "And we'll tackle it first thing tomorrow morning."

"I'm a'comin', Fiona," he said that night after failing to kill meat and having to settle for weak cornmeal soup. "I'll be there with you tomorrow night . . . or for sure the next. Just forty-eight hours and you'll finally be in my arms again. Ain't nothin' on earth that can stop me now."

4

The morning came chill and icy along the edges of a nearby stream. Having grazed all night again, Joe's new team looked fresher and a little rounder so that every rib wasn't showing. That was good because he wanted them to look their best when they got to the bottom of this long grade and entered the Mormon settlement.

Joe hitched the team and studied his heavy cargo of planed timber. It was all pine, but still of the highest grade, and he wondered exactly how much it was worth and what it would bring in cash or perhaps trade. Maybe he would have to take his lumber on to Carson City or even up to Virginia City to get a good price. Mormons were fair, but it was Joe's experience that they were exceptionally shrewd bargainers. Joe checked the wagon's brake and took a deep breath. The brake wasn't as strong and sturdy as he'd have liked, but it would have to do until they reached Genoa.

"We'll take it slow," he said to himself as he tied the little mule to the back of the wagon and climbed up onto the driver's seat.

The team was a bit fractious, which was surprising given how much they had suffered lately. But it just went to show you that man or beast, if treated kindly and fed well, could make an amazing recovery.

The downhill road looked clear and the view was spectacular. Joe halted his heavy wagon at the top of the grade and admired the green swath of the Carson Valley just below, and then his smile faded when he looked farther east toward the barren Pine Nut Mountains of Western Nevada. He had crossed that country once, but he'd never do it again. A drier, more hostile land he'd never seen anywhere in the West. Nevada was mostly rocks and sage, with plenty of snakes and Paiute Indians eager to lift a white man's scalp. No, sir, he would not cross the badlands of Central Nevada again.

He released the wagon's brake and started down the grade, which, at first, didn't seem all that steep. But he judged that the valley was at least two thousand feet below, and that told Joe that there were going to be plenty of switchbacks and steep places where he'd really have to be careful. Maybe he should have cut a big pine log and used it as a drag, but he didn't have an ax or log chains and he was in a hurry.

Down and down they crept, the team walking stiff-legged and afraid and Joe leaning hard on the brake, causing the wagon to sometimes go into a scary skid. But he was handling it. Joe had learned the hard lessons of freighting in Santa Fe, and he knew how to handle a team and overloaded wagon as well as any man. But this was going to be touch-and-go given the fact that his team was too light and his lumber-hauling wagon far too heavy.

"Easy now, boys! Just go easy and we'll stay to the safe side here and make 'er all the all the way down."

Joe was straining, and so was his team, when they had gone about a half mile down the treacherous and narrow grade only to come upon a big eight-mule team pulling a tall, but empty wagon up the grade.

"Give way, damn you!" the man driving shouted. "Move over to the side!"

"No, sir," Joe shouted. "I'm loaded heavy and. . . ."

Joe didn't get to finish as the mule skinner cracked his whip and his big animals lunged forward, crowding Joe and his wagon to the very edge and then . . . Joe's heart stopped as he felt the two outside wheels slip over the side.

"Hey!" he shouted, desperately trying to move his team out of danger. But the wagon was tilting and it was too late. With a sickening crunch of a wheel and then a terrible moment of wavering balance, the wagon rolled. Joe watched in horror as the wagon tongue snapped and yet his team was pulled over the side as everything lurched and spun.

He let out a holler, and the last thing Joe saw or remembered was the grinning face of that mule skinner and the sound of his whip cracking like a shot as the lumber wagon went into a sickening tumble pulling the team over the side with the sound of cracking wood and screaming horses.

After that there was a dizzying spin, a stab of pain, and a crushing of his chest before absolute darkness.

He woke up in a bed and stared at logs neatly chinked into a low ceiling. Joe's first response was to get up and move, but when he tried to rise from the bed, he gasped in agony and the darkness closed in around him like a black tunnel just as it had before.

"Mister?" the sweet voice of a woman said

a long time later. "I heard you speaking, more like calling to someone named Fiona. Is she your wife? Can you tell me who you are and who she is so that I can get word to her how bad you've been hurt?"

Joe Moss opened his eyes and saw a handsome woman with strong, high cheekbones and long, brown hair wrapped in a neat bun on top of her head. She had an expression of deep concern in her eyes, and wore a man's faded shirt and pants. There were squint lines radiating out from the corners of her chestnut-colored eyes. Her face was tanned and her lips were cracked. Joe knew at once that, when young, she must have been quite a beauty, but time and tough years had changed her so that she was now more strikingly handsome than beautiful.

Joe tried to speak and found it difficult. He heard himself croak and his hands fluttered helplessly at his sides. He hurt all over and felt like a weakling.

"Here," she said, raising a glass of water. "I'm going to lift your head just enough that you can swallow. Don't worry about spilling any. You've been doing that for weeks. I didn't think that you'd live when I found your wreck down in the canyon, but you have and that's a miracle of God's making."

Joe tried to smile, but failed. He let the

woman cup his head in her hand and then pour water into his mouth. The water was sweet and cool like her comforting manner.

"Where am I?" he wheezed, swallowing hard. "And what . . . what about my team and my wagon?"

"They're lost over the mountainside about two miles up the grade," she told him. "Three of the animals that were hitched lived, but they were injured almost as badly as you."

"Which ones lived?"

"The Appaloosa is hurt least. There's also a little mule that wore a saddle. We thought he was finished, but he's come back not much worse for wear. The beast is still lame, but he'll mend. And there was a gray horse that we got out of the canyon along with you. It's going to make it but had a lot of deep wounds. The others . . . well, I'm sorry but it was a mercy to put them out of their pain."

"You had to shoot them?"

"Yes, I'm afraid I did."

"What about the wagon and the lumber?"

She shook her head. "The wagon rolled many times and is a complete loss. Your lumber is scattered all down that steep mountainside. Some of the men in Genoa wanted to try and retrieve it for themselves, but the Mormon elders said that would be thievery unless you gave 'em permission."

"I won't do that," Joe said, his head and mind clearing fast. "That lumber is valuable. What about . . ."

"Your money, weapons, and personal belongings?"

"Yes." Joe braced himself for a big loss. He'd had a lot of cash and that would be a powerful temptation to anyone.

"I have it here hidden under my flooring. I collected it while the men got you and the stock that could climb out off the mountainside. Don't worry, nothing was stolen."

Joe was almost overcome with gratitude. With his cash he could make a rapid recovery and all was not yet lost. "Ma'am, I am much beholden to you and I'll pay you well for your kindness."

She smiled without joy. "I did not do this for payment, sir. I did it as a Christian. And I'll take no repayment, except for maybe to replenish what you and your stock have eaten. But that will be a small amount, I promise."

Joe nodded with appreciation, and then he remembered the mule skinner that had pushed him and his outfit over the edge. "There was a mule skinner that did this to me, ma'am."

"What do you mean?"

"I mean that I was run off the edge of the mountain by a murderin' mule skinner."

Her eyes widened and she shook her head. "Surely it must have been an accident."

"It wasn't, ma'am. And if I ever. . . ."

She gently but firmly placed a forefinger over his lips. "Sir, please do not tell me that you have vengeance in your heart. That is a very dangerous and treacherous road you were coming down and you are not the first person to have gone over the edge . . . although you are the first one to have lived to tell about it. But more to the point, you are alive because of God's miracle. And to swear vengeance against someone after being saved . . . well, it would be a travesty against the Lord. So forgive and forget. You have your money, which is considerable, and some livestock still as well as your life. Surely you must feel a huge debt of gratitude and understand it would be wrong to have revenge in your heart."

Joe Moss could see that she was upset and completely sincere. She was also about the closest thing he'd ever seen to being a living saint. And because of what she'd done for him, he knew that there was no good purpose to be gained by telling her about that dirty, sonofabitchin' mule skinner who'd done him so wrong. But if the day ever came when he met that man, well, it would be the day that one of them died.

"You are right, ma'am. It *is* a miracle that I'm alive. And I won't speak of that foul act again."

"Good," she said with relief. "There is far too much anger and hurt in this world. It poisons the heart and the spirit. Forgive and forget is always the best thing to do."

"I would like to get up and get dressed," he told her, not even sure if he could sit up, but determined to make a stab at it. "Where are my clothes?"

She again shook her head. "Sadly, your buckskins were torn from your body and were rendered useless."

"I got no clothes to wear?" He was crestfallen because it was not an easy thing to replace buckskins in this day and part of the country.

"I appreciate your loss," she told him. "However, the good news is that you're about the size of my late husband and you can wear his clothes . . . if it suits you. If not, you can pay to have clothing made by a good seamstress in our Genoa. Or I can make you clothing, although I am not as clever with needle and thread as our seamstress."

Joe wasn't real happy with any of those alternatives, but resigned himself to the idea of wearing a dead man's shirt and britches. "I'll pay you for your late husband's duds, I reckon."

"They are a gift."

Joe could see that she would not take his money for her late husband's clothes. "Ma'am, what do you do?" he blurted out. "I mean, besides saving folks that go over the side of that mountain."

She squared her fine shoulders and lifted her chin. "I am the widow of a very successful farmer."

"Children?"

Her smile melted into sadness. "Mr. Johnson and I were not so blessed. But he left me with a very nice farm, good house, and excellent livestock so I make do without hardship."

"Are you . . . are you a Mormon?"

She looked away quickly and tried to hide the pain in her eyes, but Joe saw it shining through. And then she whispered, "I . . . don't know."

The answer confused Joe and he stammered, "It's none of my business." He felt ashamed of himself for asking such a personal and obviously painful question.

"Oh, you'll find out sooner or later, and it

might as well be from my lips as from those of a gossiper. The truth, mister. . . ."

"Moss. Joe Moss."

"The truth, Mr. Moss."

"Joe. Just Joe," he said.

"All right. But I would prefer that you call me Mrs. Johnson."

"Yes, ma'am."

"My first name is Ellen, but I think that . . . given the circumstances here, it would be best if you called me Mrs. Johnson."

She was blushing, though he had no idea why.

"Anyway, you will soon learn that I am an . . . an outcast from the Church."

"Why would that be?" There he went again, asking a question far too personal.

"I was afraid that would be your next question," she said, appearing to want to choose her next words very carefully. "The truth is that I have been ordered to marry an elder in this community. Mr. Eli Purvis is a good and upstanding man of property who is very much respected."

"But you don't want to marry Mr. Purvis." It was not a question, really. Joe wasn't the brightest man in the world, but it was clear by her expression that Ellen did not care for Purvis despite his social status and wealth.

"That's correct," she slowly answered. "I don't love him and never could love him despite his fine personal qualities, his godliness, and high standing in this little farming community."

"That's a pretty good reason not to marry someone," Joe said, trying to be encouraging.

"Not if your Church orders you to do it," she replied, a trace of bitterness in her voice. "Mr. Purvis, you see, owns the section of land next to my own. The Church believes that our two farms, if joined, would be three times more productive. Also, Mr. Purvis . . . well, he rather fancies me . . . though I cannot imagine why."

Joe finally saw a chance to brighten her day a little and he grinned. "Why, Mrs. Johnson, it's because Purvis has good eyesight! With all due respect, you are a *very* handsome woman. You'd be a prize even if you were penniless."

She blushed, and actually swiped a hand across her pretty face as if batting at a gnat. "I swear, you are a *flattering* man, Mr. Moss."

"Joe."

"Oh, yes, Joe. Well," she said, clapping her

hands together. "Let's not talk about that anymore."

"Just one last question." Joe had to know. "Mrs. Johnson, if you continue to refuse to marry Mr. Purvis, what will happen?"

"I don't know yet," she said honestly. "These are good people. Blessed people who care about one another. But now that I have gone against the wishes of the elders, I am not one of them in spirit anymore."

"But you would be if you married Mr. Purvis?"

"Oh yes! I would be . . . hmmm . . . how can I say this? I would be redeemed and held in high regard again."

"Do they taunt or mistreat you?" he asked.

"No! Of course not. It's just that my life is now rather . . . lonesome and quiet. I have much to do here. Too much, really. But I am grateful for that because when you are very busy and tired, you don't think so much about the past or the future." She stood and laced her fingers together. "Now, can we talk about giving you a bath?"

The question caught Joe completely off guard. He didn't know what to say because he was so flabbergasted.

"Mr. Moss. Joe," she said when his discomfort only heightened. "You haven't had time to look, but you are completely undressed under that cover. I had no choice but to bandage and clean your wounds, which are many and serious. I'm afraid that your hip appears to be broken. Also a foot that is only now starting to heal and which I think was crushed. I thought that your left arm was broken as well, but now that the swelling has gone down, I don't think so."

"I am in some pain," he confessed. "And I haven't yet tried to move."

"I wouldn't move if I were you for a few more weeks."

"More weeks!" Joe gulped. "How long have I been here?"

"Five weeks."

He groaned. "And I'm still. . . ."

"You are still very much in need of time and rest. If you try to move now, you may damage yourself and undo what healing has begun."

"But I can't stay here."

"I don't see why not. The tongues have been wagging since I found you, and they won't stop until long, long after you leave."

"Ma'am, I sure am sorry."

She lifted her chin. "I have prayed every night and every day about this and I believe you are my salvation."

"Huh?"

"Salvation," she repeated. "Did you ever

hear of Rachel in the Holy Bible?"

"No, ma'am."

"Well, if you had you would understand. Don't you read the Bible, Joe?"

"I don't read. Period."

"How sad. Maybe I can teach you before you leave."

Joe didn't know what to say.

"Now, about that bath. You are, Joe, smelling rather ripe."

He blushed. "And that ain't good."

"No," she answered with a smile. "That ain't good."

"Could I do it on my own?"

"You can try."

"Then try I will if you will give me a basin of water and soap."

She placed her hands on her hips and nodded. "Good. You are not a lazy or fearful man, Joe."

"Mrs. Johnson, the truth is that I've never been much afraid of anything."

"Except the Lord."

Joe didn't want to tell her that he didn't spend a minute a month fearing the Lord, but he decided that would not be to good purpose, so he said nothing and, after a few moments, she turned with a shake of her head and went to heat his bathwater.

5

If it hadn't been for him wanting so bad to find his sweet Fiona, Joe Moss would have greatly enjoyed his slow convalescence in the little shed out in back of Mrs. Ellen Johnson's farmhouse. The truth of the matter was that Mrs. Johnson was a wonderful cook and she would read him stories . . . but only on the condition that he at least learn the alphabet, then read and write a few simple words. After all, she explained, and like it or not, he was going to be convalescing for at least two more months.

"I've never been one for much schoolin', Mrs. Johnson," he told her, on his way to making an excuse not to learn reading. "My pappy and mammy couldn't read nor write and they figured it was just a waste of time."

"Nothing against your parents, Joe, but they were wrong. A person who is literate has the key to a world of knowledge and wisdom passed down from others who came before him."

"Mostly, what I learned was passed down in stories told down through the generations," he replied. "Simple word of mouth, like the Indians have used for longer than the white man has been here bossin' him around."

"Yes, I understand the importance of oral history and learning," she said with great patience. "*However,* there are many things that you can learn from people that you will never know because they either lived in another time or in a distant and interesting place."

Joe puzzled over this for a few moments, then said, "No disrespect, ma'am, but I can't see what some fella livin' in another time or place could teach me that would make my life easier."

"Oh, but that is not the least bit true!"

She left the room, and returned a few minutes later with an old and yellowed newspaper. Opening it, Ellen Johnson studied the articles for several moments before saying, "Here's something you might find interesting. It is an article in the *San Francisco Times* about a man who invented a new rapid-firing and revolutionary weapon."

"Powder or cartridge?" Joe asked suspiciously.

"I'm sure it's cartridge, and this says that it was designed by Richard Jordan Gatling, who was given the patent."

"Never heard of him," Joe said dismissively. "Is this Gatling feller from east or west of the Mississippi River?"

"I imagine east of the Mississippi," she replied. "Anyway this gun has six barrels and. . . ."

"Six barrels!" Joe scoffed. "Hellfire . . . oh, excuse me, ma'am, but I don't see how any man could aim down more'n one barrel."

"Well, that may be true," she said, "but this one has six and they revolve around a central axis permitting an extremely high rate of fire."

"How fast?"

"Over a hundred rounds a minute."

Joe scoffed. "Ha! How's any man gonna even pull the trigger so fast, much less hit anything? Why, that weapon is a fool's dream. Ain't worth nothin' to nobody."

"Perhaps yes and perhaps no," she said. "But here's an interesting article on the War Between the States concerning aerial photography."

"What?"

"Aerial photography," she repeated. "It says that the Union Army has now used aerial reconnaissance carried out by a balloonist named Thaddeus Lowe, who photographed Confederate ground emplacements around Richmond, Virginia, at an altitude of one thousand feet."

Joe's jaw dropped. "A man went up in a balloon a thousand feet so he could photograph Johnny Rebs?"

"That's what it says."

"Well, why didn't they shoot him out of the damned sky?"

"I don't know."

"See there?" Joe said, with a triumphant look. "First you tell me about some fella that invented a six-barreled gun that couldn't hit the broad side of a barn. The next minute you read about another fella that was dumb enough to go up in a balloon and get himself shot out of the sky unless he was mighty lucky or the Johnny Rebs were poor shots, which I heard is not often the case."

Ellen Johnson gently folded the newspaper up and set it aside. "I can see that you are a difficult man to reason with and not likely to change."

"I'm no child, Mrs. Johnson. I've made more than my share of mistakes, but I like to think that I've learned a bit from each of them."

"And now you're going up to the Comstock Lode to find Fiona."

"If she's still there and will have me, then I'll take her for my wife."

Ellen nodded. "Well, I do hope she is there and that you and she get married and live happily ever after."

"The boy, too," Joe blurted. "Well, maybe the little jasper is a girl. Still, I'll take either one and do my best to raise 'em straight and provide for them well."

She studied him closely, and then asked, "Are you willing to be a deep-rock miner, Joe Moss?"

"Don't know nothin' about minin'," he admitted. "Especially deep-rock. I have panned a little for gold, yet never found a trace. That said, I'll still do what it takes to feed and provide for Fiona and my child."

"That's very admirable," she answered, smiling, "but I wonder if you have any idea of how awful and dangerous it is to go down in those deep mine shafts and try to dig for gold and silver."

"Can't be any more dangerous than when I was trappin' beaver up in the land of the Blackfoot and they was always after my scalp."

"I'm sure that is true. But in the mines the dangers are of a very different kind, and I can't quite imagine a man like you working far down under the earth with a pick and shovel."

Joe thought about that for a moment and agreed. "I'll do it if I must. But first I'd sure try hard to find something better. Besides, I might even start my own business."

"Doing what?"

"I dunno. But I've got a wagonload of lumber scattered down your mountainside that I mean to collect. I can either sell that lumber or use it to build some kind of business."

"Joe, do you remember anything about that mountainside where you went over?"

"Nope. Only that it had to be real steep."

"That may be an understatement. The mountainside is not only steep, but strewn with boulders, bushes, and even pines. It will take a huge effort to retrieve that lumber . . . perhaps more than you can offer."

"I'll get that lumber if I have to carry up every board on foot," Joe vowed. "Once I'm back on my feet and get my strength, I'll do it before the first snows of winter."

"I hope you can," she told him. "Because everyone agrees that it will be warped and ruined by next spring after lying under deep snow for months. They say that what isn't broken or splintered is green and needs seasoning."

"I reckon that is so."

"Where did you buy it?" Ellen asked. "From a mill up on Lake Tahoe?"

"Yes, ma'am." Joe felt awful for lying to this good Christian woman, but he thought it was the better thing to do than to admit that he had been forced to kill two freighters and that the lumber was not really his own.

"It must have cost a great deal to buy that much lumber and I certainly hope that you can recover your investment."

"Oh, I'm sure that I can," Joe said, wanting to change the subject. "So what else did that newspaper tell you?"

"I didn't think you'd want to hear any more, given your reaction to the two articles I read."

"Maybe I was a mite too quick to judge," he admitted.

"Well, I'm afraid much of that newspaper was given over to accounts of the great War Between the States," she said, "which is entirely sad and depressing. But I do have books in the house and I will read a little of them if you are interested."

61

"Sure am."

"But first, let's go over the alphabet and then the spelling of your name."

"Oh, ma'am!"

"Joe, please."

Hell, how could he deny this woman who was his savior anything? "All right, ma'am."

And so for the next two hours they worked on the alphabet and his name, until Joe started to get the hang of it. Letters were like sticks in a beaver's dam. Each one, by itself, wasn't worth nothing. But put together just right, they formed a word. And one word added to another word formed what this widow woman called a sentence. And when you added a bunch of sentences, you had a paragraph, and that all told you something important.

"I appreciate the way you explain things. Once, when I was a boy, a schoolmarm came to our cabin and caught me out in the fields working. She asked if I'd like to go to school and I said I reckoned that I would. But then she talked to my folks, and they both said they reckoned I didn't need to learn anything from her that they couldn't teach me themselves."

"And that was the end of it?"

"Not quite. The schoolmarm seemed to take me on as a special cause, and she kept

62

coming around with books and primers and such. They had pictures and the alphabet. And I snuck 'em into the woods and looked at 'em for quite some time."

She listened with great interest. "And then what finally happened, Joe?"

"My pappy caught me lookin' at them books and he skinned my behind with a willow switch till I couldn't sit down for a week! He put them word books in a feed sack and slung 'em over the cemetery's fence, and I don't know what happened to 'em after that. I do know that the very next time he went to town, he looked up that schoolmarm and he musta gave her billy-be-damned because she never came by again. Got married a few years later and went off, but the settlement found another teacher."

"I was the schoolteacher for Genoa before my husband died, so your story touches my heart," Ellen said after a long pause during which she seemed to reach back into her past and find pain. "Believe it or not, there are still parents with the same attitude your parents held. And there is nothing as sad as a wasted mind, Joe. Nothing in the world as sad."

"I reckon not," he replied, not at all sure of what she was talking about but believing she was right about learning and the mind.

"Can Fiona read and write?" Ellen asked, suddenly changing course.

"Sure can," Joe answered proudly. "She and her mother used to read the Bible most every night on the wagon train. And her father read from the Good Book when Fiona's dear mother died on the trail of a fever."

"That must have been very hard on them both."

Joe frowned. "It was terrible hard on Fiona. But her father is the kind of man that don't know what he lost even when it's gone. He's a big, braggin' sort who drinks too damn much . . . not that I haven't gotten drunk many a time myself and am fit to judge . . . but Mr. McCarthy is the kinda man I'd just like to kill."

"Joe!" Ellen cried with shock.

He realized at once that he'd upset her. "Only a figure of speech, ma'am."

She studied him closely for a moment, then said, "There is something I have to ask you. And, frankly, I'm not sure that I want to know the answer."

He didn't understand. "If you want the truth, I'll give 'er to you. If you *don't* want the truth, then I'll figure that out by your expression and I'll tell you what I think

64

you'd want to hear."

Joe paused. "That's about the best I can do for you, Mrs. Johnson."

"If that is how it would be, then there isn't really much point of me asking about that bag of human scalps they found on the mountainside and threw away, is there?"

"They tossed my scalps!"

"Yes. Now what I *won't* ask you is how they came to be in your possession."

"Fair enough," Joe said with relief. He was not about to reveal to her that he'd once killed six Piegan Indians single-handedly and earned the vaunted nickname Man Killer, which he was still called in the north high mountain country.

"But," she continued, choosing her words with care, "I do have to tell you that those scalps have turned the entire Genoa settlement against you, Joe. They have been the cause of even more gossip than my taking care of you out here in this shed."

Joe thought about that for a long moment and said, "I realize now that you have gone way out on a limb for me, Mrs. Johnson. Too far out on a limb, I reckon. And I promise you that I will make sure that you are rewarded . . . whether you want to be or not, and that I will leave as soon as is physically possible for me to leave. And finally, I

65

am sorry for the trouble and gossip. I know how it can affect a woman because it hurt Fiona something terrible on our wagon train."

"Gossip is the Devil's tongue working overtime. But Joe, I was already an outcast the moment I refused to marry Mr. Purvis. And he still comes around because he is a very persistent man. He vows that he will take none other than me for his next wife."

"*Next?* Oh, yeah, I forgot the Mormon men sometimes take a lot of wives. Some Indians do that, too, you know." Joe grinned. "As for me, I couldn't handle more than one woman. No offense, ma'am, but they can be a powerful bother and distraction at times."

Ellen laughed out loud. "Was your beloved Fiona a 'bother and distraction'?"

Joe saw the trap he'd stepped in, but he was caught and had no choice but to be honest. "I reckon she was a big distraction and my downfall on that wagon train. You see, I was with her the night that Indians came and stole a few of our horses."

"You were out walking and talking."

"We were doing a little *more'n* that," Joe confessed, feeling the heat rise in his cheeks. "But the long and short of it is that those horse-thievin' Indians killed poor Tommy

66

Kramer and Fiona's arm got broken. So that's why they fired me and found another wagon master."

"I see."

"I didn't argue any about gettin' fired. I deserved it and I'm ashamed about it. But most of all, I'm ashamed for what I did to Fiona."

"You mean putting her in a motherly way."

"Sure, and us not being married."

Ellen nodded. "I hope that you find her and your child on the Comstock Lode and that everything turns out well for you as a family. But. . . ."

"But what, ma'am?"

"But she might have remarried, Joe. Or is engaged or fallen ill and died. There are many things that could have happened since you saw her. And most likely of all, she may hate you for what she had to go through."

"Hate me?"

"Yes," Ellen said. "Hate you. So be prepared for that."

Joe expelled a deep breath. "I never thought about that hate thing."

"Well, it's probably not going to be the case so don't worry about it. All I'm trying to say is that you need to be prepared for some disappointment. Life just never turns out exactly the way we want . . . or expect."

"Yes, ma'am," Joe said as the dark clouds settled in his mind. "But right now, all I can do is to get well again and then collect that lumber on the mountainside."

"That's right, Joe."

She was about to say more, but suddenly a blocky man appeared in the doorway. Ellen Johnson turned and, in the half-light, Joe could see what he was sure was pure fear pass across her face.

Joe's eyes jumped to the big, bearded man blocking the doorway, and he knew without asking that this was Ellen's overbearing and determined suitor, Elder Eli Purvis.

"Ellen, am I interrupting something *personal?*" the man challenged.

Ellen stood up straight and lifted her chin. "Of course not, Mr. Purvis. We were just discussing . . . the weather."

"Ah, I see. Well, the weather is fine as anyone can see, but how is your friend who collects bloody scalps?"

She took a deep breath and replied, "Mr. Moss is mending."

"Slowly," Purvis said. "Too slowly."

Ellen's cheeks reddened and she snapped, "Mr. Moss has a broken hip and a crushed foot in addition to some very serious cuts and bruises. And he is not a young man, Mr. Purvis."

"No, I can see that."

Purvis was in his mid-fifties. Big and strong with chin whiskers and thin gray strands of hair stretched across an otherwise bald head. His brows were black and bushy, and he wore heavy boots and baggy pants with a heavy canvas coat smeared with dirt and manure. His hat was black and flat-brimmed, and Joe's overall impression was that he was above all else a self-important and humorless man.

Joe pushed himself up in his bed and glared at the intruder. Purvis had staked out the fact that they were not going to be on friendly terms. He'd made that more than plain from his sharp words and expression of disgust and disapproval. Joe saw no reason to try to be cordial with this man who was causing Ellen Johnson so much fear and worry.

"You'd be Mrs. Johnson's neighbor," Joe said. "I'd be Joe Moss."

Purvis didn't bother to move any closer, much less shake hands. "So how did you happen to run your team off the side of that cliff, Joe? Were you drunk or just not paying attention?"

Joe's jaw clenched, and it was all that he could do to remain civil out of respect to Mrs. Johnson. "I was run off the road by a freighter comin' up the grade."

"Oh, really? Well, that's a first. I took four strong men down there and dragged you and what stock survived out of that canyon. Took us a full day away from our farms and own chores."

"I'm grateful to you for that," Joe said grudgingly.

"And in repayment," Purvis said, "we are willing to take that broken and splintered lumber."

"I'm planning on bringing that lumber back up to the road and taking it on to sell in Carson City or on the Comstock Lode."

Purvis didn't like that even a little bit. His jaw clenched and he said, "Then how will you repay our community for the loss of our time?"

Joe reckoned he should have seen that one coming. Charity toward strangers might exist in Mrs. Johnson, but it sure didn't in the rest of these people toward an outsider. "Will twenty dollars do?"

He could see that Purvis was surprised by the sum. Men worked in the nearby Comstock deep mines earning three dollars for a ten-hour day, and farm labor often brought only a dollar a day, while Joe had just offered four dollars each to the five men.

"It will do," Purvis said. "Providing it is

payment in gold and not federal dollars."

"It will be."

There was a long silence, and then Purvis asked, "Are you a man of God?"

"I reckon God made us all," Joe said. "And that includes Indians."

The man's eyes widened. "Heathens are not Christians and they'll go to hell."

"Judge not lest ye be judged, Eli Purvis," Ellen said, coming between them. "And now, I have my own chores to do if we're finished talking."

Purvis was being dismissed, and he didn't like that from how his eyes tightened at the corners. He gave Joe one last withering look of disdain, and then turned and walked away.

"I can see why you'd not want to marry that man," Joe said. "How many wives does he already have?"

"Three."

"I feel damned sorry for 'em," Joe told her. "You'd be better off stayin' single than marrying a man like that."

"I know, but I might not have a choice in the matter for much longer."

Joe blinked. "Why not? You and your husband owned this farm."

"That's true," she replied, "but without help and if no one will buy my eggs, milk,

71

or vegetables, I'll have no income and they'll force me under."

Joe didn't doubt that she was telling the truth. "Well," he said, "I'll help you starting tomorrow. I'm about ready to get out of this shed and move about. My hip feels half-mended and my foot is a trial, but I can use a crutch and still get from here to there. Say, you wouldn't have a little whiskey to ease the pain of it would you, Mrs. Johnson?"

She almost smiled. "Joe, you *know* that I wouldn't."

"Yeah," he said, trying to hide his disappointment. "But it never hurts to ask, ma'am."

When Mrs. Johnson was gone, Joe dressed and eased himself out of the bed. His broken hip hurt so bad he nearly passed out, and he could only put a little weight on his foot, which was still swollen and purple.

But he'd had his fill of lying in bed as an invalid. He would get to work and do whatever he could to help this woman, and he'd not once complain or whine about it, either. Because as long as Joe Moss was around, Eli Purvis might as well suck rope rather than think he could bully or force Ellen Johnson into becoming his fourth wife.

6

In his first few weeks upright, Joe had to rest more than he worked. But he did his best to help Mrs. Johnson, and he could split firewood pretty well standing or seated on a log. Within days of his decision to get up and get to work, Joe had made a crutch from an aspen and Ellen padded the crosspiece that went under his arm with a piece of lamb's wool. She did that despite Joe's protests that he didn't need things to be sissified.

The Johnson farm was 160 acres of good, flat land, and it was cross-fenced and irrigated from a gushing stream that came down from a canyon and ran right through Genoa. The stream was used by every family and the amount of water was fairly allocated. Mrs. Johnson, for example, was allowed all the water that she could use for eight hours every fifth day. When it was her turn to use water, Joe and Ellen would go out into the fields and open and close wooden gates flooding the farm's ditches and pastures.

"Mighty good water and grass," Joe said one fine afternoon as they watched the mountain water pour across one of the pastures. "This is a fine piece of land, Mrs. Johnson. You ought to grow corn and more hay like your neighbor Purvis."

"He's got a lot of help given his wives and all those children," she said. "It's all that I can do to raise a big garden, feed the livestock, pigs, geese, and chickens."

"I suppose that you could sell this place for a good amount of money."

"No, I could not," she countered. "Only a Mormon would buy here. Anyone else would be frozen out and their water would be stopped. And no Mormon will buy from me because it is understood that I am to be Eli Purvis's wife."

Joe's mouth turned down at the corners. "God didn't give this land to the Mormons or anyone to hold forever. The Paiutes had it first, and long after Purvis and the rest of us are dust, this land will be used by others. We can't really own land, ma'am; we can only just take care of it while passin' through life."

Ellen's sunbonnet was pink as were her

cheeks this day, and several strands of her long hair had slipped loose so that she cut a fine and pretty picture in her fields. Now, she smiled and then laughed. "Why, Joe Moss, I declare that you are a bit of a philosopher!"

"Is that bad?"

"Not at all. It shows me a part of you that I didn't know existed. Are you reading those words that I asked you to learn in the evenings after we take supper?"

"Yes, ma'am." He felt sorta proud about it. "I can spell *dog, man, woman* and *run, jump,* and *bone* all fine, thank you kindly. And I've been practicing writing my name until it looks less and less like chicken scratches."

"Good!"

Ellen leaned on her hoe, and they both watched the clear mountain water flow across the grassy pasture. She turned her face up toward the Sierras, which seemed so close and tall that they looked ready to fall right over the top of them. "I do love this land, Joe Moss. I was raised on a farm outside of Baltimore. The earth was rich and giving, but it was an entirely flat land with not a mountain or even a hill in sight. I would sometimes try and try to see the earth curve from our porch, but I never did.

I sometimes thought the earth was flat rather than round, although I had been taught better. But here with the Sierra Nevada so big and close and tall . . . here you almost think you're halfway to heaven."

Joe slipped his crutch out from under his arm and rested his whiskery chin upon it as he followed her gaze upward toward the peaks. "Have you ever been up to the lake, ma'am?"

"I have," she said with a soft smile. "When my husband first brought me here, we went up to the lake and spent two glorious summer days. We fished and swam . . . oh, my goodness, is that water clear and cold! But I have never felt so clean and fresh. I would like to go up there and visit it again someday, but . . ."

"But what?"

"I have the livestock to tend and they depend on me. I couldn't just leave them."

"No," he said, "I reckon not. And I suppose your neighbors wouldn't be willing to feed 'em."

Her eyes fell from the mountaintops and she stared at the grass with a sad shake of her head.

Joe hobbled over to a gate and diverted the water into the next pasture. "What is the date, ma'am? I have sorta lost track."

76

"It's August. I think it is the tenth of the month. Why do you ask?"

"I need to go up there and start collecting my lumber," he answered. "When will the first snows fall in this country?"

"They usually wait until October . . . maybe a little earlier or later."

"Then I've got to get up there soon," he told her. "And do you know what I'm going to do with the first load I bring down?"

"I have no idea."

"I'm going to build you a fine two-seater."

"Joe Moss!" She acted embarrassed.

"Not so we could sit side by side and hum 'Dixie,' " he said with a bold wink. "Just so you'd have a nicer one than Eli and all his wives and children. And I'll make sure it has no cracks or drafts. It'll be a thing of rare beauty in these parts. People will come from all around to admire your new two-seater."

Ellen burst out laughing, and gave Joe a gentle push that almost sent him sprawling to the grass. "Joe, you are almost hopeless!"

"Almost is all right," he said with a chuckle.

And then they went to work moving water and Joe could hear Ellen humming "Dixie" in the soft summer breeze.

■ ■ ■ ■

"I would like to hitch up your wagon to the Palouse and my gray horse and then go up the grade and bring back some lumber," Joe said a few days later.

Ellen just stared at him. "I don't think you are up to that, Joe. The mountainside is very steep and . . ."

"Well," he said, a little irritably, "I've got to see it for myself and give'r a try. I just can't wait any longer to start collecting that lumber."

"Very well," she said, "but I'm going with you."

"That's not. . . ."

"It is necessary," she told him. "To have any chance at all, one person will have to be up on the road while the other goes down on a rope."

Actually, that's the only way that Joe had figured it could be done. "I'll go down," he said, "and when I tie some lumber up, you can get the team to drag it up the side. When we got a light load up on the road, I'll come up and we'll bring it down here slow and easy."

"Are you sure that you don't want to wait a little longer?" she asked.

78

"No, ma'am. I have to start now. If it don't work, then it don't work. But I have to try."

"All right," she said, "then we'll rise before the sun and do chores, then leave. It's only a couple of miles up the grade and we can be there just after daybreak."

"Good," Joe said. "And I'll pay you for your help."

"You already paid Mr. Purvis and the others twenty dollars. I think you should hang onto your money."

"I never liked to hang onto money for long," he admitted. "I feel that it is made to be spent, and I can't think of a better way to spend it than to give some to you for your kindness."

She was pleased. He could tell that she was very pleased. "I could very much use some cash."

"Then it's settled. I paid those Mormons each four dollars a day and I'll pay you the same, if that's agreeable."

"It is more than fair. Thank you."

Joe had to look away because, dammit, he was the one that owed Ellen Johnson more than he could ever repay.

"So we'll get to bed early," he said quietly. "Because tomorrow will be hard."

"Yes, but I still expect you to do your studies before you sleep."

79

"But, ma'am!"

"Study, Joe. You promised me that you'd learn five new words every day."

"I overreached," he told her.

"No, you didn't. And tomorrow we can have a spelling lesson on the way up the mountainside."

"Now that's a right fine idea!" he said, not quite managing to hide his sarcasm as he hobbled off to the shed.

7

To reach the grade, they had no choice but to drive Ellen Johnson's rattling buckboard through Genoa, and even though the sun still wasn't fully off the horizon, there were a few early risers who saw their passing. Ellen and Joe both called out a greeting, which wasn't returned.

"I didn't stop to think how much grief this is going to cause you," Joe said with deep regret. "I'll be leaving before the month is out, but you'll have to stay and live with these stiff-backed people. From the feelin' I'm gettin', that won't be easy."

Ellen sat beside him on the buckboard seat, her face wrapped in a shawl because of the early morning chill. "Don't fret about that, Joe. I was an outcast when you arrived and I'll be one long after you've left. It's your lumber up on the mountainside, and what we need to do is to worry about getting it up to the road and onto this wagon.

The rest will take care of itself."

"I expect that's true," Joe said as they passed through the little settlement and then started up the steep grade.

Joe's Palouse and gray horse were teamed with a pair that Ellen owned, and even though the wagon was empty, it was a hard climb and they had to stop and let the animals blow every half mile. But at last they reached the place where Joe had been forced over the side. Joe set their brake and climbed down to gaze at the steep mountainside.

"Ain't much left of that wagon, that's for sure," Joe said, shaking his head. "I can't believe any of my livestock survived."

"*You* almost didn't," she reminded him.

Joe studied the wreck and the lumber strewn up and down the slope. There was clear evidence that some of the lumber, which had spilled closest to the road, had already been scavenged by passersby. It was only the lumber that was scattered several hundred feet or more down the slope that remained.

"Have you thought about how you're going to do this?" Ellen asked. "Because it looks utterly impossible."

"We've got rope," Joe told her. "I'll go down and tie up some boards; then you ask that mule we've tied behind our wagon to drag 'em up. When we get a full wagonload, the mule will pull me up and we'll call it a day."

"Are you sure that you're up to this?" she asked, making clear her skepticism. "I mean, your hip isn't fully mended and your foot is still swollen and purple."

"I'll do it," Joe vowed. "Let's quit jawin' about it and set to work."

Without another word, Joe got the ropes out of the wagon and tied them together and then around his waist. "Wrap your end around the wheel a couple of times and just play out the slack as I work my way down," he ordered. "It'll go fine."

Joe went over the edge and started down. The slope was steep and rocky and the footing was awful. So bad that he kept falling, and he was glad that Mrs. Johnson couldn't see the struggle he was having. But foot by tenuous foot, Joe was making his way down and using every shrub and little tree that he could grab to keep from falling more than necessary.

At last Joe came to a pile of lumber that was stacked about like if you'd tossed a pitchfork of straw into a loose pile. There were boards aiming in all directions, and he found it hard to untangle them and then get them pointed up and down the slope. When he had a half dozen eight-to-ten-footers lined up, he shouted, "Pull 'em on up!"

It worked just fine for the first part up the slope, but then the lumber got snagged on a big bush, so Joe had to fight his way back up the slope and get the tangle straightened out. He was gasping and in pain, but determined to get a load this day.

"Okay! All clear! Pull 'em on up to the top now!"

This time the lumber slid over the lip of the road above, and in no time at all Ellen Johnson was standing on the edge looking down. "I'm going to throw the rope back, but I don't know if it'll go all the way down to you!"

"Do your best."

The rope, of course, didn't go all the way down to Joe, so he had to scramble back up to reach it, then drag it down for more lumber. It took them all morning to drag up maybe fifty boards, and some of those were splintered and probably not worth the effort.

"Pull me up!" Joe shouted when he was so tired and in so much pain that he could no longer stand.

The little Mexican mule was probably

almost as weary as Joe when he was dragged onto the road and lay gasping in pain and covered with dust.

"I don't think this is worth it," Ellen said, looking at the small number of boards she had stacked on the edge of the road.

"I'll do better tomorrow," he promised. "But I think I've about done all that I can do today."

"Maybe we could hire help."

"Who in Genoa would help?" he asked.

"No one," she confessed.

"Then we'll do it ourselves and I'll pay you for your time, Mrs. Johnson."

"All right," she said quietly. "We'll have to go up a little higher to find a place to turn this wagon around. Then we'll load the lumber."

"Sounds good," he gasped, biting back the pain radiating from his hip and crushed foot.

"No, it doesn't sound good, and I'm not a bit sure that the lumber is worth the pain and effort. But you know what?"

"What, ma'am?"

"I'm going to hold my head up high when we drive back through Genoa so that those folks don't know how tough it was this morning. And that we aren't going to quit until every last stick of lumber is retrieved."

Joe had to grin despite his pain. "You've got a lot of grit and spunk, Mrs. Johnson. I like that in a woman."

"I like it in a man," she said. "And after what we've been through, Joe, I think it's high time that you just started calling me Ellen. To heck with what anybody thinks."

"Does that mean I can move out of your shed into your bed?" he asked, barely able to keep from laughing.

"You try it, Joe Moss, and I'll put a whole lot more hurt on you than you're feeling now!"

Joe looked at her face, which was covered with dust-streaked sweat. *By gawd,* he thought, *I'd better get that lumber up and sold and then move on to Virginia City before I start thinking ungentlemanly thoughts about this spunky woman.*

For the next three weeks they kept to the same hard routine. Get up way before dawn and do the milking and the chores, then hitch the wagon up and saddle the Mexican mule and tie him to the back of the wagon. Then it was on through town with the same disapproving faces and expressions coming from the Mormon townspeople. Ignoring their icy disapproval, Joe then drove up the grade, and then climbed down the side of the mountain tied to a rope.

Joe fought the pain, and he went farther and farther down the mountainside each day, until he had all the lumber that he could reach by tying together every rope that they could lay hands upon. He supposed, if he spent a day and went to Carson City, that he could have bought more rope and gone deeper into the steep canyon, but the lumber down there had fallen and tumbled so far that it was mostly worthless.

"That's it, Ellen," he announced one day when they'd loaded the last that could be recaptured. "Some of it probably ain't worth no more than firewood, but a lot can be cut and trimmed and will bring a good price up on the Comstock."

"I'm sure that's true," she said as they turned the wagon around and then loaded it for the trip back through town to her farm. "So when do you think you'll be leaving?"

"Soon," he told her. "No sense in putting you out anymore. I'd like to fix a few of your fences and split more wood and get. . . ."

"No," she said too abruptly. "I'll do those things. Joe, I've put some thought to it and I think it would be best if you left tomorrow."

"Tomorrow?"

Somehow, Joe hadn't really been thinking of rushing off. He and Ellen had become close, and his lessons had taken on some flavor now that he'd progressed to the point where he could read more than a few simple words. Why, he'd even taken to reading some of Ellen's old newspapers, and he'd picked up considerable information about a world he'd never known and would likely never see.

"You've got a son or daughter you've never seen up there in Virginia City," she quietly explained. "And you need to get up there and make your peace with Fiona Mc-Carthy."

"I doubt that's her last name anymore," Joe said, feeling troubled. "Seeing as she has already married and been widowed once."

"Well, that may or may not be the case," Ellen said, her lower lip quivering slightly. "But you've pinned your heart on having her and you need to go and find out if that's going to happen."

"I'll miss you," he blurted out, picking up the lines and slapping the team too hard.

"Shut up and don't say anything more," she told him with a shine in her eyes. "Just . . . shut up and drive."

Joe swallowed a lump in his throat and

headed on down the grade with his final load of salvaged lumber. He should have been mighty happy to be leaving. It would only take him two days to be at Fiona's side . . . but he found that he was feeling sad and low.

Sometimes, he thought, a man didn't know what the hell to think when it came to the confusing mysteries of the heart.

8

Ellen Johnson was a strong woman both physically and mentally, but she hadn't been prepared for losing Joe Moss. It had, of course, been far harder to lose her husband because they'd been married for sixteen years. And although they'd sure tried hard enough and often enough, the Lord had not seen fit to bless them with children, so they'd only grown closer with each passing year. And despite or more likely because of being childless, they'd worked even harder to take a piece of bare land and transform it into a fine and profitable farm. In fact, they had thrown themselves into such a fit of working from dawn to dusk that they'd often been reproached by the Mormon elders for neglecting their church duties.

In response, Ellen and her husband had always countered that they were laboring for the Lord and that their profits only increased their tithing to their Church. And when it came to tithing, the Mormon elders had not seen fit to criticize or encourage the industrious Johnsons to work less and pray more.

But now with her husband gone, and then with Joe coming into her life so completely dependent on her nursing and loving care, Ellen found that there was a vast, empty place in her heart that made it ache from morning to night.

"Joe wasn't the man that my husband was in many ways," she whispered as she fed her pigs and chickens, "but there were things about him that I cannot forget. He was illiterate and probably had killed men and had many women . . . but still, there is a simple goodness and courage in Joe Moss that I cannot deny. And despite his rough language and ways, Joe has a strength that more than matches my own . . . an attribute that my husband did not share."

There were days when Ellen Johnson felt so sad and lonely that she could hardly force herself through the day, and then she felt guilty for not working harder. Often, she pushed herself to her absolute physical limits so that she would not have the time or energy to think about Joe and how he had gone away to find the love of his life . . . Fiona.

"I hope he finds her and it goes well for him up on the Comstock Lode," Ellen often told herself, trying to believe those words. "And that he has a fine son or daughter that will soften him and make him wiser. And I'm glad that I had the time to share with him and give him some book learning. Joe Moss, though he might not fully realize the fact, left my farm a far better and more knowledgeable man than when he had arrived half-dead."

Ellen told herself these things a thousand times a day to buoy her troubled spirits, but even so, she missed Joe all the time and the pain in her heart would not go away.

She was weeding the garden one morning and working up a good sweat when Elder Eli Purvis arrived in his buggy dressed in his Sunday clothes. Ellen was so busy attacking the weeds with her hoe that she did not even hear or see Purvis arrive until he had driven into her yard, scattering her flock of chickens.

"Good morning, Mrs. Johnson!" he called, smiling grandly and removing his hat to reveal his baldness. "You are working too hard again today."

Ellen leaned on her hoe and surveyed the devastated weeds that she'd just chopped, trying to think of a suitable response.

92

Finally, she was able to muster a half smile and reply, "Yes, there is much to do while the weather holds."

"Too much for a woman of your age."

Ellen felt her hackles rise. She was, after all, considerably younger than Mr. Purvis and . . . she would bet . . . far fitter. "I'm not *that* old, sir. And I am plenty capable of hard work. I've done it all of my life."

Purvis could see that he had misspoken and angered the woman, so he placed his hat back on his head and forced an even wider smile. "Of course you're not old! In fact, you are a remarkable specimen of womanhood. Strong, smart, and industrious."

Ellen did not know how to take a compliment from such a man and she had her suspicions as to his motives. "And how are your wives, Mr. Purvis?" she asked. "I have not seen them in quite some time even though we are all neighbors."

"They are well and happy in my home, thank you."

My home? she thought. Of course. With these Mormons the home and the property all belonged to the man. If a woman wronged that man, she could be excommunicated from the Church and the society and would receive absolutely nothing for her years of labor and devotion.

"I'm glad to hear that, Mr. Purvis."

"Yes," he said, momentarily seeming to be at a loss for words. "Uh, well, I was wondering if you would like to go for a nice little drive over to Carson City today. I know that you have not been out for a good while and thought that you might need to do some shopping."

"How thoughtful of you," she said. "But I have enough supplies until the end of the month. And I really do need to finish weeding this garden. I've already let the weeds go too long."

"All work and no play," the man said, trying to hold onto his fading smile. "Really, Ellen, I insist that you take a day off and accompany me to Carson City. You look rather tired and a change of scenery would be good for your mind and body."

Ellen did not want to go for a long wagon ride with Mr. Purvis for she knew that he would almost immediately badger her about them getting married and joining their farms. On the other hand, she had found herself looking to the north thinking of Joe Moss and of other people living in different ways. And she had not been to Carson City in months. Perhaps she could manage to squelch Eli's talk of marriage and anger him into silence, then enjoy the change of scenery.

"Well," she said, "maybe you are right, Mr. Purvis. I could use some coffee, beans, and calico."

"Excellent!" he said, beaming. "I will water these horses and wait for you by the barn."

"I'll only be a few minutes," she promised.

"That mangy fellow that you took in for a while left rather suddenly, didn't he?"

"That's true," Ellen said, turning away so that he could not see the pain in her eyes.

"Good riddance, I'd say," Purvis continued. "He was a freeloader and none of us can understand why you helped him retrieve that lumber."

"He paid me very well," Ellen said, because it was true and she knew that money was something that this man would actually understand.

It took Purvis a moment to recover before he said, "Money isn't everything. And considering the shame that you brought upon —"

Ellen didn't let him finish and her eyes flashed with anger. "Shame, Mr. Purvis! *What* shame!"

Purvis reeled back as if he had been slapped. "Well, I mean . . . I mean it wasn't

95

really . . . proper."

"Damn being proper!" Ellen stormed. "I'm a Christian woman and I did a Christian act in helping heal that man. And I don't care what you or anyone else says, I am proud of my actions."

"Why . . . why, of course you are, Ellen. But that man was not our kind and he was a heathen. Everyone could see that."

Ellen could feel blood pounding in her head. "Mr. Purvis, I think that you had better just leave. You have greatly angered and insulted me as well as the Lord."

"Now just a minute, woman!" he thundered. "Take care how you speak to me."

"You're on my land and I'll speak to you as I please!" Ellen was trying hard not to start crying out of frustration and deep anger.

Purvis bowed his head for a moment, fists clenched at his side. Finally, and with great effort, he raised his head and looked at Ellen. "Forgive me," he croaked. "You are right about it being a Christian act of kindness. And although I don't understand why you allowed the man to stay so long or why you helped him collect that lumber . . . what is past is past. And you do look exhausted. Please, come with me to Carson City. I will treat you to a meal in a restaurant and we will speak no more of Joe Moss."

"Is that a sworn promise, Mr. Purvis?" she demanded.

"Yes, a sworn promise."

Ellen took a very deep breath, and it occurred to her that if she sent this man away, it would be looked upon by him and those he told of his invitation as a small, but important victory. In Genoa, it would signal the first crack in her armor. A sign of weakness.

"All right then," she said, "I will get ready and we will go. But if you do not keep your promise not to mention Joe Moss again, then I will never again be in your presence."

He took her at her word and her threat made him stand up straight and square his still-broad shoulders. "When Eli Purvis gives his word on a thing, it is as good as gold."

"Good," she said, savagely swinging the hoe at one last large weed and sending it flying through the air.

9

Ellen Johnson knew that Carson City, nestled in Eagle Valley and backdropped by the Sierras, was the new territorial capital of Nevada. But much to her surprise, Eli Purvis turned out to be somewhat of a local history buff and knew even more about the town.

"It was originally settled in 1851, not long after we arrived to found Mormon Station, now Genoa," he said on their way to the capital. "Carson City was named after Fremont's scout, Kit Carson, though I think that they could have found a far more admirable character. Some of our people think we should buy up land in Carson City while it's still relatively cheap. But I don't. The land there, as you know, is dry and mostly covered by sagebrush. The Carson River is too far to irrigate the land profitably."

"I never got the impression that Carson

City could be a farming community," Ellen replied. "Being the new territorial capital and now that the Comstock Lode is booming nearby, its future must surely be commerce and government. And isn't the new legislature meeting at the Warm Springs Hotel just east of town near the Carson River?"

"That's true," Purvis grudgingly admitted. "The town fathers are also building a railroad called the Virginia and Truckee up to the Comstock, and I understand that the government is constructing a United States Mint. You see, with the War Between the States raging back in the East, the Union and President Lincoln are pushing very hard to bring western territories like Nevada into the fold. But there is lawlessness and corruption in commerce and government, and already Carson City is becoming a wicked and sinful place."

"I never thought it sinful or wicked," Ellen countered. "I think it's a rather nice town. But I have heard that Virginia City is quite wild."

Eli Purvis glanced sideways at her. " 'Wild' is an understatement, Ellen. Satan rules the roost up there on Sun Mountain. The entire Comstock Lode is one big den of sinfulness. And that is why it was no surprise to learn that it was the destination of Joe Moss."

"Have you ever been up to the Comstock Lode?" she asked, deciding to let the insult pass because she was in his wagon and it would be a long walk back to her farm.

"No, of course not! Why would I subject myself to that kind of sinful place?"

Ellen shrugged. "Just wondering."

They were quiet for a few minutes, then Purvis said, "As I said earlier, there is a strong push to give Nevada statehood and I think that Carson City will be its new state capital."

"Statehood," she said, smiling. "That would be very important and change everything in this part of the country, wouldn't it?"

"For some," he said vaguely. "But it wouldn't affect our town."

"Are you so sure?"

"Of course!" Purvis looked upset and blustered. "As you know, we protect and serve only our own."

Ellen could not have failed to detect the emphasis this man placed on his last three words, or the very obvious reference to her unpleasant situation.

Before she could think of a reply, he added, "And you *are* one of our own, are you not, Ellen?"

Momentarily at a loss for words and filled with foreboding, she remained silent with her hands clenched in her lap.

"Dear Mrs. Johnson," he said, sensing a moment of vulnerability, "why are you making things so hard for yourself? If we were wed . . . and our farms combined . . . we would become the biggest and most successful farm in Genoa. And our houses. . . ."

"*My* house!" she cried.

"Yes, your house," he said soothingly, "would remain your house. Perhaps you would enjoy the company of my Rebecca and her two daughters and . . ."

"No," she blurted out. "And I do like and respect all of your wives, Mr. Purvis, but I will not live with them."

"That would be perfectly acceptable, I think. However, your property and my property would be joined. And there is one more very important consideration."

"And that is?"

"Children," he said flatly. "Your late husband was no doubt a fine man, but sadly infertile. I, as is obvious, am not."

Ellen turned on him with her cheeks turning red. "Mr. Purvis, could we please not talk about this now? I am tired and I need to think about what I should buy in town."

He wasn't pleased, but he was smart enough to sense that he had pressed the issue as far as she would allow. "Of course. Let's just have a pleasant outing and not speak of serious things on such a fine day."

Or any day, she thought, wondering for the thousandth time if her late husband had been infertile . . . or if the curse was hers alone.

Carson City had enjoyed tremendous growth just since Ellen had been there last. Now she saw the new United States Mint was under construction and that many new homes and businesses were springing up like flowers after a good rain. The street was filled with wagons and the sidewalks crowded with pedestrians. Ellen gazed at all the activity with real interest, and noted a new millinery store as well as a butcher shop and dry goods store. The women on the street were dressed with color and wearing lovely hats and bonnets. The men all seemed quite dapper as well compared to Eli Purvis and the churchmen of Genoa.

"Where do you want to shop?" he asked. "I need to go to see the blacksmith."

"Anywhere is fine," she said, not wanting him to be able to find and accompany her before she had completed her shopping and was fully ready to leave.

Purvis drew up his team and then consulted his pocket watch. "I will help you load your purchases," he told her. "Will an hour be enough time before we meet at the Ormsby House for lunch?"

"Make it two hours, Mr. Purvis. I do have a considerable amount of shopping to do and I'm grateful for the opportunity. Besides, we've come too far to rush ourselves, don't you agree?"

He did not agree, but she was climbing down from the wagon and already waving good-bye over her shoulder before he could protest.

I wonder if by some faint chance Joe Moss is here, she asked herself. *I would recognize the wagon I sold him to haul his lumber, but I doubt that he still owns it. And why would he still be here? He's up in Virginia City with his beloved and their child. Oh, well, smile and enjoy this visit because it could be your last in quite a while.*

10

Joe Moss was feeling real good. He wouldn't need to drive Mrs. Johnson's buckboard all the way up to Virginia City because he'd sold that old wagon, all his livestock except the Palouse, and every last stick of the recovered lumber in Carson City for a hefty amount of money. He'd been a little sad to let his good Mexican mule go, but he'd gotten a fair price and the liveryman in Carson City had warned him about the high cost of boarding animals on the Comstock Lode.

"Hay up there is higher'n hell," the man said. "You'd be better off selling me your Appaloosa gelding and taking a stagecoach up to Virginia City."

"Well, that's probably right," Joe told the man, "but I just wouldn't feel right without a horse to ride. And while we're on the subject, I'll be needing a new saddle, horse blanket, bridle, and lead rope. Oh, a pair of good saddlebags."

"You could buy 'em new at the saddle shop," the man told him, "but I'll sell you everything you need at half the price."

So Joe bought himself a new outfit, and then while he was in the spending mood, he went and got a hot bath, shave, haircut, and some new clothes and boots. "Sure you haven't got any buckskins around that'd fit me?" he asked the handsome young tailor.

"No buckskins," the man said with an easy smile. "Nobody wears them anymore except a few old mountain men and Indians."

"Well, *I* was a mountain man," Joe told the man. "And I trapped beaver in the days when a beaver pelt was worth plenty."

"Mister, you don't look old enough to have done that."

"I started at a young age," Joe replied. "Those were good days when the streams were full and there was an annual rendezvous up along the Green River. Back then you could buy a pretty Indian girl for less'n what it'd take trappin' in a month. And I bought more'n a few."

The tailor blushed with embarrassment. He was a tall, gangly fellow with straight red hair. Joe figured that he would one day fill out to be an impressive man, and wondered why he'd chosen to be a tailor. "What's it like up on the Comstock Lode?"

Joe asked.

"It's crazy is what it is," the tailor answered, taking a few quick measurements. "Everyone has money in their pockets, but they spend it like there's no tomorrow. The town is wild and dangerous. I'd like to go up there and open a business."

"Then why don't you go?"

The young man shrugged. "I'm trying to save up some money. I don't really enjoy this work. What I'd really like to do is gunsmith. I've a talent for it and I've won a few shooting contests here in Carson City. I work on people's weapons whenever I get a little free time."

"Is that a fact?" Joe said, more impressed with the young man than he'd been before.

"It is." He stuck out his hand. "My name is Redford Wallace. But everyone just calls me Red."

"Red, do they have any law up there in Virginia City?"

"Nope. The only law on the Comstock Lode is the law of the jungle. The strongest, quickest, and smartest are the rulers."

"Well," Joe said, liking what he heard, "I'm still plenty strong and quick. As for being the smartest, I'll have to pass on that one. But I can read and write a little."

"Is that a fact?"

"Yes, sir," Joe said proudly. "It *is* a fact. Always could do the numbers. A man who can't add and subtract is going to get cheated every time."

Red finished his measurements and stood up. Their eyes met on the same plane, telling Joe that the young man was about six-foot-two.

"How long is it gonna take before you can stitch up my new pants legs and sleeves on this coat?"

"I can have them ready for you in about an hour," the young man replied.

"Fair enough," Joe said, peeling bills off a thick roll. "I'll be back for 'em shortly. There's a few dollars extra for you, Red, for puttin' on the speed."

The tailor was probably only about twenty and when Red saw Joe's roll of greenbacks, he couldn't help but stare. "You've got quite a bankroll there, Mr. Moss."

"Yes, I do. I'm going to buy me a new rifle and scabbard soon as I find what I like. But first, I'm dyin' for a few shots of good rye whiskey."

"I'd recommend the Lucky Lady Saloon just up the street. They'll serve real good liquor, if you tell them that is what you want instead of their usual cheap rotgut."

Just then Joe spotted a new Stetson up on

a high shelf. "If you got any of those that fit me, I'll take one."

"They're twelve dollars and fifty cents," Red told him. "Let's see if we can find one your size."

Minutes later, Joe left the tailor's shop and stopped in the window of a store to admire his new boots and hat. He also had a haircut and a shave, and barely recognized himself.

"Fiona is gonna think you've gotten a lot younger and handsomer," he said with a chuckle as he made his way along the boardwalk whistling an old and familiar tune.

The Lucky Lady Saloon was much to Joe's liking, and when he asked for the "good stuff," he was given a full bottle of John Bull.

"Be four dollars," the bartender said.

"That's kinda steep, mister." Joe leaned on the bar. "And what if I don't drink the whole bottle?"

"Then you put the cork in it and take it with you," the bartender replied. "You buy a bottle here, then it's all yours."

"Fair enough."

Joe again produced his huge roll of greenbacks and counted off the money. The bartender was suddenly a lot more impressed with Joe. "You passin' through or stayin' for a few days?"

"Passin' through on my way up to Virginia City," Joe told him. "Reckon I can make it if I leave in an hour on a real good horse?"

"Even on a good horse you won't get that far before dark."

"I ain't afraid of the dark," Joe said.

"I'm sure you're not. But why don't you stick around until morning and then go?"

Joe waved aside the glass that the bartender pulled up from under the bar top. "If it's all mine, I can drink 'er from the bottle without a glass."

"I expect you can," the bartender said. "Say, why do you wear a tomahawk at your belt along with that big bowie knife?"

Joe squinted and put on his most serious face. " 'Cause you never know when you might have to split a man's skull open who insults or tries to cheat you. And then, just for good measure, I'll take his scalp."

The bartender was shocked and threw up his hands. "This is a *friendly* place."

"That's good because I prefer to be a friendly man," Joe answered. "But should someone cross me, I'll kill 'em without thinkin' about it even the once."

"I'm sure you would," the bartender said, wiping a sudden sheen of sweat from his brow.

Joe grinned and uncorked the whiskey. Closing his eyes, he sighed with anticipation and then he raised it to his lips and drank swallow after wonderful swallow. His eyes filled with happy tears and his throat and belly warmed up like hot coals in a campfire. When he set the bottle on the bar, it was down by a third.

"Holy cow, mister! You sure kicked the hell outa John Bull! I haven't seen many men that could put down that much whiskey without taking a breath."

"I could pour the whole damn bottle down my gullet, if I had a mind to. And I might just have a mind to," Joe said, feeling the heat spreading down until his toes tingled and tapped on the sawdust floor.

"Well, I know you have the money and I've got as much whiskey as you want to drink," the bartender said. "So . . . if you're of a mind to get drunk . . . don't hold back."

"I am of a mind," Joe decided. "I haven't had a good drunk in the longest time, and I believe a man needs to go on a toot once in a while in order to keep his innards clean and workin' right."

"I couldn't agree more," the bartender said with a wide grin. "Drink up!"

Joe did drink up. He drank that entire bottle, and then he paid another four dollars and bought a second. By then, his head was spinning lazy circles like the flies around the tin ceiling and his world had a rosy hue. Joe and the bartender were laughing, and so were the fellas all around him that he was buying drinks for. It was a hell of a good time and before Joe knew it, the daylight was gone and he was having a little difficulty standing at the bar.

"You need a room?" the bartender, whose name turned out to be Willard, asked. "We rent upstairs rooms."

"I probably could use a little food," Joe said.

"I'll send a boy for a plate. Beef stew and corn bread all right?"

"Sounds top-notch," Joe said, burping and taking another drink.

The beef stew didn't arrive until Joe and his new friends were finished with the second bottle and working hard on a third. But what the hell, it was only twelve dollars, and it had been the longest time since he'd been on a drunk and having so much fun.

Joe told his new friends all about his mountain man days, and then about leading that ill-fated wagon train west, and when he came to Fiona, he found that there were tears in his eyes and leaking down his

111

cheeks into his beard. So he corked the bottle and squared his shoulders like a man. No blubbering woman was he, by damned!

"But I'm going to find her tomorrow," he announced to his drinking friends. "I got a fine set of new . . . hiccup . . . clothes paid for and . . . hiccup . . . waitin' so I'll look good when I find her. I want Fiona to remember me as the man she was meant to marry."

"Let's drink to Joe and his future bride!" the bartender shouted to the room as more men came to crowd around him. "Mr. Moss, how about one more round for the boys!"

They were all looking so eager and happy that Joe didn't have the heart to refuse them, so he bought a fourth bottle and it was gone quicker than he could count off another four dollars.

"I guess I'd better take that . . . hiccup . . . room," he said, gripping the edge of the bar. "You got any jerky or tobacco?"

"I sell good cigars and bad cigars. The good ones are from Cuba and the bad ones smell and look like burnt dog shit."

"I'll take a Cuban," Joe said, trying to remember to remember to buy a corncob pipe, which he preferred to smoke.

"Wise choice."

112

"And that room and some help gettin' up those stairs to it."

"Sure thing, Mr. Moss. Room is ten dollars."

Joe was grinning, but now his face turned hard and ugly and his hand fell to the tomahawk. "Mister, you must think that I'm either stupid or out of my . . . hiccup . . . mind drunk to pay ten dollars!"

"The room I had in mind comes with something special," the bartender said, backing up fast.

"Ain't nothin' so special in a room worth ten damn dollars!"

"Whatever you say, Mr. Moss. Five dollars?"

"Three is more'n fair after all the drinks I just bought." Joe peeled off three dollars and shoved his bankroll back deep down in his pocket.

"Three is fine, Mr. Moss." The bartender turned to a man in a white shirt and tie. "Charley, would you please help Mr. Moss up to Room Fourteen?"

"Sure thing." Charley was big and beefy. He grabbed Joe by the arm and started to steer him away, but Joe didn't like anyone grabbing him so he threw off Charley's grip. "Just point the way," he growled.

"There are the stairs," Charley said.

"Think you can make it up them?"

"Watch me," Joe said, placing one new boot in front of the next, only to discover that he was listing badly.

Everyone that had been drinking Joe's expensive John Bull laughed, and that made him mad so he whirled around and grabbed a card table for support, fumbling for his tomahawk. When he finally got the damned thing out of his belt, the men stopped laughing and grew silent.

"You people . . . hiccup . . . drink a man's whiskey and then you make fun of him? Is that how it's done in these parts?"

Nobody said a word and nobody was smiling anymore as Joe waved his tomahawk around, and then let out a wild Indian whoop and began to dance a bit on the barroom floor. Suddenly, he was remembering a time up along the Green River when he was this drunk and about to get into a fight with a mountain man named Crazy John. They'd both had tomahawks and Joe thought they were just funnin' around and having a good time. But then Crazy John had taken a swing and struck Joe on the forearm, cracking the bone. It hadn't hurt too badly then, but it had made Joe mad and he'd whacked Crazy John in the shoulder, opening up a gusher of blood and shocking even the riotous rendezvous crowd. For a moment, it could have gone in either direction, one man killing the other. But he and Crazy John had started laughing and then shaken hands. They'd been good friends right up until the day that the Blackfoot had captured and scalped Crazy John.

The Lucky Lady Saloon suddenly began to roll under his feet, causing him to fall on the floor. He tossed his beef stew and liquor into the sawdust, and then wiped his mouth with his sleeve, soiling his new shirt.

"Mister, why don't you put that tomahawk back in your belt and let Charley help you upstairs?" the bartender asked.

"Maybe I will," Joe said, grabbing a chair and climbing to his feet. "And maybe I'll have me another bath tonight."

"Might be a good idea before you meet that woman."

Joe puked a little more and smoothed his fouled shirt. "Enjoyed the company," he said, lurching for the stairs. With Charley's reluctant assistance, he finally made it to his room and collapsed on the bed.

"You puke all over this room and it'll cost you another dollar," Charley warned. "If you're gonna puke some more, then I'll help you down to the end of the hall or have a

Chinaman bring up a slop bucket."

"I'm done now," Joe said, sitting up and closing one eye so that Charley wasn't a pair of Charlies.

"You sure can drink and tell windies," Charley said just before leaving. "I'd guess that you were a real heller in your younger days."

"I'm *still* a heller," Joe slurred.

"I'll bet your guts are shot," Charley told him. "A man that can drink like you has been doin' it for a while and has to have rotten guts."

Joe grabbed his tomahawk and was ready to see if he could nail Charley between the eyes, but the man ducked out of the room and ran down the hall.

After that, Joe lay on the bed and fell asleep. Soon, he dreamed of his mountain man days and those unbelievable rendez-vous when all of his trapper and Indian friends would get together and trade, drink, and fornicate like wild weasels. They'd run footraces, wrestled, fought, and gambled for stakes that had taken the best part of a year to earn. And they'd swapped Indian girls, told outrageous lies about strangling grizzly bears and running down elk on foot and then riding them bareback over the high mountain peaks. Oh, what a time that had been!

Now dreaming and snoring like a resting steam locomotive at the station, Joe felt like those fine times had happened a whole 'nother lifetime ago . . . and he guessed that they surely had.

Hiccup.

11

Joe Moss awoke deep in the night to feel someone tugging at his pants. Instantly, he knew that they were trying to get at his roll of bills, which was half of all the money he possessed.

"Hurry up!" a voice urgently whispered. "Get it and let's get out of here."

"I'm tryin', dammit! Man, he sure stinks!"

"Shut up and get that money!"

Joe was just sober enough to realize that he had to act fast or he was going to be robbed or maybe even murdered. His bowie knife was still in his belt and so was his tomahawk, so Joe grabbed the thief's wrist in his left hand and his bowie knife with his right. He stabbed the thief just below his rib cage and then twisted his blade upward.

The man let out a horrible scream and Joe felt his warm, spurting blood. The second thief jumped on them both because he was still determined to get Joe's bankroll.

Joe couldn't get the first man off himself and was trapped by the weight. Suddenly, the bed slats broke under the three of them and in the confusion and blood, Joe rolled sideways and then was rolling on the floor.

The light was poor, but Joe recognized the second man to be Charley. A muzzle flash exploded between them and Joe felt a bullet graze his neck. He'd lost his bowie, which was slick with blood, but he still had the tomahawk, so he pulled it free and slashed at the dim outline of Charley's face just as the man fired a second shot that went wide.

Joe's tomahawk glanced off Charley's head, shearing off an ear. Charley yelled and Joe rolled onto the man, slamming a fist into his face and then grabbing Charley by the hair and bashing his head up and down on the wooden floor. Charley tried to gouge out Joe's eyes, but that stopped when Joe began hacking the man's scalp from his skull.

"You sonsabitches drank my whiskey and then tried to rob and kill me!" Joe raged. "I'll have *both* your scalps!"

Charley was hysterical as Joe chopped off his scalp and then buried the blade of his tomahawk in the man's forehead, splitting it open like a ripe melon.

Joe crawled over to the first man. It was the bartender. "You bastard!" he shouted, pulling his knife from the man's body and then scalping him while he quivered and his heels tattooed the floor. The bartender wouldn't stop screaming until Joe cut his throat, and even after that he continued to make the most awful sucking sounds.

By now, everyone in the upstairs rooms of the Lucky Lady was pouring out into the hallway and then filling Joe's doorway. Someone had a lantern and when they saw Joe waving two bloody scalps, one of the men began to puke out his guts even harder than Joe had done earlier.

"Jaysus Kee-rist!" a man whispered, his eyes wide with pure horror. "I've never seen anything the likes of him!"

"That's Charley and Willard's scalps that he's waving!" another gasped, before choking and turning away to be sick.

"Get him!" someone growled.

Joe was still drunk and quite proud of himself for the fight he'd won when the mob in the doorway came down on him like a mountainside.

"Where the hell am I?" Joe groaned, feeling as if his head was about to explode.

"You're in the Carson City Jail."

120

Joe tried to focus, but his head was pounding and one of his eyes was swollen completely shut. When he tried to cradle his aching head, he realized that his wrists and arms were shackled. Suddenly enraged, he shouted, "What is going on here!"

"Moss, there are witnesses that will swear you slaughtered and then *scalped* two of our citizens and *you're* asking the questions?"

Joe took several deep breaths, and then he managed to see a blocky man wearing a badge standing in front of him with other men crowded behind. He glanced down at his pants and saw at once that the roll of bills was missing. "I've been robbed!"

"You are being held for murder."

Joe couldn't believe what he was hearing. He struggled in vain against his shackles, then got control of his temper. "Sheriff," he said, looking up at the hard-faced official, "as God is my witness, I was sleeping it off in my room when those two men started beating and trying to rob me. I just fought back and killed 'em, that's all. And now my roll of money is *gone!* Take these shackles off and let me find out who took my money! When I find 'em, I'll kill you a third thief, by cracky!"

"Mister," the man said, "I'm the sheriff of

this town and I'm the one that's going to ask the questions."

Joe had a foul taste in his mouth and asked for a drink of whiskey. But the sheriff shook his head. "Water, if you behave yourself. That's all you're getting until we decide what to do with you, Moss. We've seen what happens when you get drunk."

Joe glared up at the man. "When I get drunk I *stay* drunk until I'm ready for sleep. And I was sleeping when those two men came in to rob and murder me. Hell, I was in my own room when it happened . . . wasn't I?"

"Yeah, you were. And I'm not sayin' that Charley and Willard weren't there to rob and harm you. But the way Charley's woman tells it, you invited them both up to Room Fourteen to play poker."

"Poker!" Joe roared. "I was so drunk I couldn't even have held my cards! Charley's woman is lyin'!"

"I think that's for our circuit judge to decide," the sheriff said, folding his arms over his broad chest and glaring down at Joe as if he were a crazed killer. "Until he comes to town, you're gonna stay chained and locked up, and you'd better behave yourself or you won't get anything to eat or drink."

Joe cussed a blue streak.

"Moss," the sheriff warned, "I'm a Christian and I don't much like to hear that kind of profanity. You keep it up and it'll go hard for you. Judge Paxton is a Christian himself, and he sure won't look favorably on your case if I tell him about your foul gutter mouth."

Joe squinted up at the man and his voice was thick with fury. "Sheriff, in case you're forgettin' the facts, *I* was robbed and nearly killed in my own hotel room bed. I fought 'em off in self-defense. I deserve to be given a medal for permanently riddin' this town of such thieves and murderers. Instead, you got me chained up and my money is gone. That means someone came in *after* I killed those two and stole my bankroll. So what the hell kind of justice do you folks serve around here?"

"You scalped them!" one of the men behind the sheriff cried in a voice choked with anger. "I was there and you scalped 'em when they were both *still alive!*"

"Well," Joe said between gritted teeth, "if they were still alive when I lifted their hair, then they damned sure deserved it. If I'd have had a little more time, I'd also have cut off their balls!"

"He's an animal! Worse than a heathen

123

Indian!" someone standing behind the sheriff yelled. "We ought to just hang that inhuman sonofabitch right now! String him up and let him dance and choke his way into Hell!"

Some of the others behind the sheriff let him know they were all for that idea. Joe glared at the bunch of them wishing his hands were free and filled again with his knife and tomahawk. If that were the case, by gawd, he'd take some more scalps in one helluva hurry.

"Judge Paxton ought to be comin' through in about four days and —"

"Four days!" Joe bellowed. "Do you mean I'm supposed to be chained up like an animal for four days?"

"You *are* an animal, Moss. And until the judge comes, you'll be treated like one."

Then the sheriff turned and had to shove an angry crowd out of the jail. He slammed the door and left Joe spitting and cursing. All in all, Joe knew he'd gotten himself in one bad, bad fix. The only thing he had in his favor was that he'd buried half of his money, at least three thousand dollars, in the same stall where his Palouse horse was being boarded.

But neither that money nor his fast horse was of any help to him now. And if his luck turned as sour as the taste in his mouth, he might even get hanged.

12

Ellen Johnson was in Bergman's Mercantile Store buying some yardage when she overheard three women talking excitedly about a gruesome murder the night before and how a lot of the men in town were working themselves up to a "necktie party."

One of the women was saying that the jailed murderer was probably going to be hanged. He was described as being a tall stranger who wore a tomahawk on one hip and a bowie knife on the other.

At that moment, Ellen's heart stopped and she nearly fainted.

"Is anything wrong, ma'am?" the clerk asked from behind his counter.

Ellen took a few deep breaths and squared her shoulders as the three women went outside still talking excitedly about the "necktie party." They were giggling and carrying on as if there was a church revival or circus in town.

"Is a necktie party a lynching?" Ellen managed to ask, knowing for sure that the tall stranger accused of the murders had to be her dear Joe Moss.

"Yes, ma'am," the clerk said, eyes dancing. "And if ever there was someone who deserved to dance at the end of a rope, it's this fella. Not only did he stab Charley Packer and Willard James to death, but he also *scalped* them!"

Had Ellen been made of lesser inner stuff, she would have either fainted or gotten sick right then and there. Instead, she turned away to try to hide her face and compose herself. "I . . . I think I'll look at some more yardage," she said vaguely as she moved back down an aisle.

"That's fine, ma'am. I'll just keep this yardage you picked up here at the counter so it will be ready. It'll cost $2.15 total."

"Thank you," Ellen said over her shoulder as she managed to keep her feet moving. She made her way down to the rolls of yardage that she'd already spent time examining, and stood before them for several minutes trying to gather her wits about her.

"That green and blue floral would look real nice on you, Mrs. Johnson," the clerk said from right behind her, nearly causing her to jump a foot high. "And that beige material is also a favorite. It's on sale, too."

Ellen swallowed hard and without turning around, she said, "I'm afraid I was a little upset by the talk of those murders and a lynching. Do you know anything about this man that is accused of the crimes?"

"He's more'n accused. They caught him in the act. There is a bunch of witnesses that will swear that poor Willard and Charley were screaming something awful while he was scalping them alive."

Ellen had to reach out and support herself on a shelf of canned goods.

"Are you all right, ma'am?"

"I'm afraid not," she admitted. "I need to sit down and if you could get me a glass of water. . . ."

"Yes, ma'am! I shouldn't have said anything. But the whole town is buzzin' about those murders and I just assumed that you'd already heard all about them. Terrible thing. What kind of a man would stab to death and then scalp two men even before they were dead!"

Ellen shook her head, unable to find words and wondering if she could breathe.

"Come right over here to this chair and I'll get you a drink of water," the clerk said solicitously. "This isn't a subject that a lady ought to even hear being talked about."

Ellen bent her head and fought back hot tears. *Oh Joe, Joe,* she anguished, *what kind of demons do you have inside? Are you possessed by Satan? What did I do when I saved your life only to have you take the lives of two others so savagely? Dear God, did Satan use me?*

"Ma'am!" the clerk said, almost running down the aisle with a glass of water that was spilling on the floor. "You're crying! Oh, dear, I'm so sorry that I've upset you!"

The clerk was a man in his thirties, a good man, one of the Bergman family, and was genuinely sorry that he'd upset her so much. Ellen scrubbed her tears away with a handkerchief and forced a smile. "It's not your fault. Really, it just sounds so shocking and horrible."

"It *was* horrible. Worst murders this town has ever seen and the people are really upset. All morning I've had friends that I've known for years as being kind and gentle coming in here swearing that this man should receive rope justice. No one is willing to wait for Judge Paxton to come to town and hold a trial. People in Carson City want to deal out swift and righteous justice."

"What brought about this terrible act?" she managed to ask.

"This tall fella named Joe Moss got roar-

129

ing drunk in the Lucky Lady Saloon and bought four bottles of whiskey, drinking most of them all by himself."

"Four bottles of whiskey?"

"Yes, ma'am. Nobody had ever seen drinking like that before. Then, drunker'n a skunk, he went up to his rented room . . . it was Room Fourteen and I hear it looks like a slaughterhouse . . . and invited Charley and Willard up to play poker."

"Joe Moss doesn't play poker," she heard herself say. "He only plays three-card monte and faro."

"What?"

Ellen drank half the glass. "I said Joe Moss believes that he's unlucky at poker, so he just plays three-card monte and faro."

"How do you know that?"

"I just do," Ellen said, mind racing. "So you say that Moss invited those two men up to his room to play *poker*?"

"That's right. He must have lost because he got crazy mad and stabbed, then scalped them both."

"Was there a large amount of money found on anyone?"

"No, ma'am. I know that because the undertaker told us that there wasn't more than ten dollars between the three of them."

Ellen stood up, spilling more water.

"Here," she said, shoving the glass at the confused clerk. "I have to go visit Mr. Moss. Where is he being held?"

"At the jail."

"And where is that?"

"Two blocks up the street on the right. You can't miss it, but . . . but Mrs. Johnson, you can't go see a crazed animal like Moss!"

"I'm afraid you're wrong," she said, pushing past him and nearly racing for the door.

"But what about your yardage!"

Ellen couldn't begin to think about yardage. If Joe Moss was a double murderer, she would have to hear it from his own lips and she knew that he wouldn't lie to her. She was probably the only person in the world other than his Fiona that he wouldn't lie to.

All she knew was that Joe wouldn't play poker. He'd told her that at the farm and he'd been quite sincere about it. And being a private man, he would not have invited two strangers up to his hotel room. No, if Joe was going to get drunk and gamble, then he'd have done it all down in a saloon among men.

"Mrs. Johnson! Ellen, wait!"

She turned and saw Eli Purvis hurrying after her. He was a half block behind and because he was a big man and too heavy,

Ellen knew that he wasn't about to overtake her on foot.

So she started running up the street with tears on her cheeks and a desperate need to see and hear the truth from Joe Moss before he was torn from jail by an enraged mob and hustled off to a "necktie party."

13

Ellen ran to where a crowd of angry men and women were standing in front of the jail. Heedless of their protests, she pushed her way through the mob until she was standing in the jail's doorway and staring at the town's sheriff and several other men. In the back, behind the bars, she could barely make out Joe's battered face turned downward toward the floor.

"Hold up there!" the sheriff yelled, jumping forward to block Ellen's forward progress. "I'm Sheriff Olsen. Who are you and what do you think you're doing in here?"

Ellen wasn't badly winded, but she took a moment to say, "There's been a mistake. Joe Moss doesn't play poker and he wouldn't have invited those men up to his room. They must have gone up there to rob and kill him."

The sheriff scowled, aware that he was being closely watched by half the town wanting Joe Moss's head on a platter. The sheriff cleared his throat officiously. "Ma'am, you're one of those Mormon women that live out in Genoa. Is that right?"

"Yes, but. . . ."

"Well, ma'am, I can see you are upset and it sounds like maybe you know that murderer in my jail. That said, however, I'd appreciate it if you'd just turn around and go back to Genoa. What happened last night is *my* business and the business of this town. So please turn around and leave. This is no place for a lady."

Ellen desperately wanted to go speak to Joe. His head was hanging low and he was covered with blood. He looked even worse now than when she'd found him unconscious and all smashed up on the steep mountainside.

"Sheriff Olsen. This man is my very good friend. I was able to help him recover from a terrible wagon wreck near our little farming town, and I know that he would not do the things that he is being accused of."

"You're wrong about that," a smaller man interjected. "I'm B.J. Anderson and I'm the mayor of Carson City. Joe Moss was caught in the act of murdering two men last night and then scalping them alive. So, if he is your friend, you made a bad, bad choice. This man is going to be tried for two murders and he is sure to be hanged."

"Can I please talk to him?"

"No," the sheriff snapped.

"Just for a few moments. *Please.* He's behind your bars and appears to be hurt."

"Oh, he's hurt all right. But he's damned lucky he isn't dead. He will be before long."

"Sheriff, I have to talk to that man!"

"Why?"

Ellen swallowed hard. She was willing to say anything to get to the truth and hear what Joe Moss had to say. "Because . . . because I love him."

Olsen's mouth sagged and the mayor's eyes dilated before he stammered, "You *love* that murderer?"

She hadn't meant to blurt that out, but now that it was said, Ellen knew there was no retracting her shocking words. "Yes, I love him. And I want to talk to him in private. If Joe did what you say, then he'll tell me so. But if not. . . ."

"Ma'am," the sheriff said, his voice angry and full of impatience, "it don't matter what he says or doesn't say. I'm tellin' you that there were a bunch of witnesses standing in the door of Room Fourteen when Moss finished stabbing and scalping Willard and

Charley!"

"Please," Ellen whispered. "Just let me speak to him in private for a few minutes. It's very, very personal and important to me."

"Ellen! Ellen, for heaven sakes, have you lost your mind!"

She heard and recognized Eli Purvis, but ignored his angry yelling.

"*Please,* Sheriff."

"Oh, hell, all right. But you've only got a few minutes and I'm going to stay inside and watch you both like a hawk. And there's *nothing* that your friend Joe Moss can say that will change anything. He's bound to be hanged just as certain as death and taxes."

"Thank you."

Olsen wasn't a bit happy as he pushed and shoved everyone including the mayor out of his office and locked his front door. Then he marched over to his office chair and threw his feet up on his desk, glaring at Joe and Ellen. He took out his pocket watch and laid it on his desk saying, "Five minutes. That's all the time you can have and I'm gonna catch hell for even giving you that long."

Ellen rushed over to the bars. "Sheriff, can't I go inside and. . . ."

"Dammit, no!" Olsen thundered. "Talk to

136

that animal through the bars."

Ellen leaned close. "Joe," she whispered, "you've got to tell me what happened last night. They say that you got drunk and invited those two men up to play poker. But I remember you telling me that you hated poker. Didn't trust the game and only played three-card monte or faro. So I know you didn't invite those two men up to your room and then hurt them without a very good reason."

Joe raised his head, and she gasped when she saw the full extent of his facial injuries. "Ellen," he said quietly. "I don't know why you're here. You need to go back to your farm. I'm no good and I'm gonna hang. I *did* kill and scalp them two bastards."

"But why, Joe?"

He was silent for so long that Ellen thought Joe Moss wasn't going to say anything more, but then he opened up a little. "It's true I was roaring drunk and I went upstairs to my room to sleep it off. But those two men attacked me when I was about passed out. They had seen my roll of money and they were trying to take it away. I fought back and it got real nasty. I ended up killing them both in self-defense."

"But Joe, why did you scalp them?" she asked, starting to cry again. "I'm sure that's what has gotten everyone so upset."

Joe shook his head. "I got my blood up and I was still pretty drunk. I'd shared my liquor with them and they turned on me like yellow dogs. So I scalped them. I've done it before, but that was a long time ago and I didn't think I'd do it again . . . but I just did."

"Oh, Joe," she whispered. "If you'd have just fought back and even killed them, then I think you'd have a chance with a judge and jury. But the scalping . . . dammit anyway, Joe!"

"I'm sorry, Mrs. Johnson. After all you did for me and now you have to see and hear about this bloody mess I'm in. I shouldn't have gotten drunk, and then I just went crazy when they snuck up to my room and tried to take my money."

"So what are you going to do now?"

"Nothin' I can do," Joe said quietly. "I'm already a dead man."

"Joe, there's a woman that swears she heard you invite those two men upstairs to your room."

"She's lyin'." Joe's eyes hardened. "I'm nobody to her and Charley was her man. Why would she say he got what he had comin' just to save a stranger?"

"I'm going to talk to her. Make her tell

the truth," Ellen blurted. "There isn't any reason for you to die for defending yourself."

"Don't do it, Mrs. Johnson."

But she shook her head with determination. "I spent a lot of time and I've suffered a lot of ridicule and grief because I did the Christian thing and helped you, Joe Moss. I'm not going to let all of that go to waste . . . so long as you're telling me the God's honest truth."

"I swear I am," he replied. "Ellen, lean a little closer to these bars."

She did it without question, and that's when he told her that he'd stashed half of his money in the stall where his Palouse horse was boarded. "I want you to have that money, Ellen. Take it and leave town. If those folks in Genoa try to force you to marry Purvis, then it'll be your grubstake. Give you a fresh start somewhere new."

"I'll get the money," she whispered, "but I'll use it to help free you any way that I can."

"No," he told her. "Don't you see it plain? I'm no good. You wasted your time and your Christian spirit on a man who ain't worth savin'. So let it be and let me hang."

"And what about Fiona?" she asked, knowing this was the one thing that would turn his head around. "What about her and that child that you're searching for? If you hang in Carson City, Fiona and that child will never know that you came to find them. And even if Fiona did read about your being hanged, how is that going to make her feel? Hearing that you murdered two innocent men and then scalped them?"

"They weren't innocent!"

"That's right," Ellen said, desperate for him to see her point. "They were thieves and they were trying to rob and then kill you. And you need to be set free so you can tell Fiona the *truth*."

"You could find and tell her," Joe said, a little hope creeping into his one half-shuttered eye. "You could do it and use that money to help the three of you."

"No!"

"If you did that, I'd march up the gallows stairs with a smile and die a happy man. Ellen, I'm begging you."

He had never called her Ellen before, and that made her feel a small amount of joy. Yet, hearing his words, she shook her head. "I'm using the money to try and save your life, Joe. And if I fail, then I'll take what's left of it and find Fiona. She can have it all."

"You should have some of it, too," Joe said

urgently. "There's a lot left that wasn't stolen. And there's my horse, saddle, and weapons . . . get 'em before someone steals 'em."

Ellen lowered her voice even more. "Who do you think stole your money last night after you killed those men and were beaten senseless?"

Joe didn't know if Sheriff Olsen could overhear their whispers or not, so he took no chances as he turned his eyes to the man with the badge.

Ellen twisted her head slightly and stared at Olsen, who was busying himself cleaning his nails with a pocket knife. In a barely audible voice, she asked, "Olsen did?"

"Yeah. I had all that money still in my pocket when they hauled me downstairs and over to this jail. I was fightin' like a wildcat and Sheriff Olsen pistol-whipped me. When I woke up this morning, the roll of bills in my pocket was gone."

"Time's up!" the sheriff yelled, coming to his feet, then folding his knife and dropping it into his leather vest. "Ma'am, I hope you appreciate the grief I'm going to catch for letting you come in here and speak in private to my prisoner."

"I do appreciate it," Ellen said, avoiding his eyes.

141

"Well," Olsen said, hooking his thumbs into his belt. "I expect he lied to you and said it was self-defense."

"That's right."

"And of course, since he's 'your friend,' you believed him."

"I *do* believe him."

The sheriff shook his head with pity. "Go back to your people in Genoa and forget all about this," he advised. "It would be the wisest and kindest thing you could possibly do."

Ellen forced herself to nod her head in sad agreement. But, in truth, she had no intention whatsoever of taking this corrupt sheriff's advice.

The angry crowd outside gave Ellen Johnson looks that would have withered a field of spring flowers. But she fixed her eyes straight ahead until Elder Purvis grabbed her arm and dragged her down the street as if she were a truant schoolgirl.

"Ellen, what in God's name has gotten into you? Have you any idea what a fool you've made of yourself and how you've insulted our entire community?"

"I'm sorry."

"Sorry!" he roared. "Woman, you have disgraced us all. You'll have to do a severe penance. And frankly, I'm not sure that I want to have anything more to do with you."

Ellen was shoved roughly up onto the wagon seat. Purvis took the lines and sent the horses jumping forward with his whip. His round face was red with anger. "You have outraged our community, Mrs. Johnson. I don't know if I can abide *ever* having you as one of my wives!"

Ellen had heard more than she could stand. She turned on Purvis and in a trembling voice said, "Oh, yes, you could abide it, Mr. Purvis. Because money is your god. But don't you worry about any of this, because I wouldn't marry you if you were the last man on earth!"

He lost control and backhanded her so hard, Ellen was knocked off her seat and fell heavily to the ground. Stunned and struggling for the breath that had been forced from her lungs by the impact, Ellen lay still for a few moments. Then, before Eli Purvis could turn the buckboard around and retrieve her, Ellen stood up and walked away.

"Ellen!" he shouted. "I'm sorry. Come back here!"

But she just kept walking with her head high and her smashed lips twisted into a grim smile. She would walk to her farm, and then she would get her two horses and return to Carson City after dark. She'd retrieve Joe's horse and outfit from the livery and she'd get that buried money.

After that, Ellen wasn't exactly sure what she would do either for herself, Joe Moss, or Fiona. But one thing she did know was that she wasn't going to let a wild but innocent man be hanged.

14

It was late when Ellen Johnson arrived at her farm, and she was in considerable pain. Her lips had been smashed and the left side of her face was badly swollen. She had also landed on her hip and was limping badly. But despite her injuries, her determination to try and save Joe Moss had only grown with each faltering step toward Genoa.

Now, she wasted no time in sacking up all her cash, gold jewelry, and most precious belongings along with food and two canteens of water. She did not know if she would be returning to this farm. If she was caught helping Joe, she was sure that the town's elders would forever banish her from Genoa . . . sending her away in poverty and disgrace. They would surely take her land by force, including her house, animals, tools, and even furniture. It wouldn't be lawful, but in this place the church elders were the only law, and they would be led by

Eli Purvis, who would no doubt be enraged by her rejection and behavior in Carson City.

"It's probably just as well," she told her farm animals as she turned them free to wander off into the darkness. "When my husband died, the die was cast and my fate sealed. I either had to marry Eli and become the latest of his wives, giving him all my wealth and possessions . . . or leave this beautiful place with little in the way of worldly goods."

Ellen saddled her swiftest horse and skillfully packed her other horse as the hour became late. She could see Eli's house not far away, and all the lights in every window were blazing. He might, she realized, even now be having an emergency council meeting demanding a vote to expel her from her property and the Church.

Hurry, she urged herself, *because they might become so angry they will not wait until morning to expel you from this community.*

There were a few precious mementoes from her childhood that Ellen also packed in the big, heavy canvas bags that she draped across the second horse. She appeared, she realized, as if she were a pioneer woman setting out from St. Louis bound for California and Oregon. Well, she wasn't going that far, but who could say? Ellen wasn't sure *where* she was going next.

On her way out, she reined her horse up beside her husband's grave and bowed her head in prayer, asking for his understanding. She had never expected to leave his graveside, but she thought he'd understand because he had also not liked or trusted Eli Purvis. She hoped he would help her in whatever trials lay ahead, but she also prayed that he wasn't aware of the hardships that his death had caused her. He had been a good man and she wanted him to forever rest in peace.

"Good-bye," she whispered, setting her horses at a steady trot back toward Carson City.

It was well past midnight when she approached the stable where she knew Joe's spotted horse had to be boarded. Ellen tied her horses up in the back deep in shadows and crept into the livery barn. Fortunately, she'd remembered to bring a candle, and now it was very useful as she limped down the row of stalls until she found Joe's handsome Palouse. Ellen let the candle drip on a rail, and then set the candle down in the warm wax and waited until it was set solid. Its flickering light was poor, but enough to do what she needed to do next. The Palouse knew Ellen well, and was not at all nervous when she entered its box stall and then fell to her knees with a tablespoon and began digging frantically for Joe's buried money.

It took Ellen much longer than she expected, and she almost missed the cache because he'd placed it far to the back of the stall almost under the heavy timbers that divided it from the next stall. Once it was in her hand, Ellen took the moneybag, and then she haltered the Palouse and led it quietly out of the barn, finally tying it with her own two horses.

"So far so good. Now what?" she asked the moon.

She had wanted to track down the woman who claimed Joe had invited her Charley and the other man up to his room. But it was way too late for that, and Ellen had no idea where to find Charley's woman. Furthermore, she doubted that the woman would ever recant her lie unless she was very well paid from Joe's recovered money. And somehow, the idea of paying a liar to tell the truth just was too hard for Ellen to swallow.

That meant that there was no choice but to try to free Joe from jail either by trickery or force. Ellen paused in the back of the old barn with the three horses and offered a fervent prayer for guidance and protection. For a way to do what she had to do to save an innocent man . . . a man with whom she had foolishly fallen in love. If she were caught in the act, as she most likely would be, she might go to prison or even be abused or hanged by an already incensed mob.

Ellen had a six-gun. A good pistol that her husband had taught her how to safely and effectively use against coyotes or foxes going after their chickens. But what she faced now was far more than a henhouse varmint. What she faced now was the wrath of a whole town directed at Joe Moss.

At the very least, she thought grimly, *I'll shove this gun through the cell window so that if they come to hang him, he will be able to defend himself one last time and go down fighting. That's the only way Joe would want it, and I will live with the guilt and consequences for the rest of my life.*

Five minutes later, Ellen was standing across the street from the sheriff's office and jail. There were street lamplights and the front of the office was well illuminated.

The mob that she had seen earlier and expected now had dispersed, but there were still a few drunks talking, drinking, laughing, and arguing on the sidewalks. Two of them were having a dispute and their voices were loud, slurred with liquor, and angry. Ellen had not heard such language before, and it singed her soul to hear the profanity. But when the pair began to fight, and then tumbled into a heap punching and kicking on the ground, Ellen put that out of her mind and moved close to the jail until she could peek in through a front window.

Sheriff Olsen had been asleep on a cot, but the noisy brawl just outside his office awakened him. And when one of the brawlers pulled a derringer and harmlessly fired its single bullet at the man who was clubbing him with an empty whiskey bottle, Olsen swore and grabbed his gun, coat, and hat.

"Hey!" he yelled, bursting out of his office. "Gawdammit! I'll arrest you both!"

But the two men either didn't hear or didn't care about the sheriff. They kept fighting and bellowing. It was an awful sight to Ellen, with one man's face sheeted in blood and the other looking crazed in the lamplight.

"All right," Olsen raged as he stepped off the sidewalk and marched toward the brawlers. "I gave you warning and now you're both gonna pay!"

Ellen slipped behind Olsen and into his office through the open door. She rushed to the back of the room and crouched beside the cell. "Joe!"

He was awake. "Ellen?"

"Where are the keys, Joe? Hurry!"

"On his desk!"

Ellen ran over to the desk and found a ring with two keys. The larger was obviously the one that fit into the heavy cell door.

"Ellen, what are you doing?"

"I'm getting you out of here."

"But they'll catch you!"

It seemed to take forever before she could get the damned key to turn in the lock. By then, Joe was fully awake and pushing the door open. He kissed her, and she almost cried out in pain because of her damaged lips. He recoiled, "What —"

"Never mind! Let's just get out of here!"

"Not without the money Sheriff Olsen stole along with my gun, tomahawk, and bowie knife," Joe growled.

"No! I uncovered the other half of your money, and your horse and mine are waiting behind the livery. Joe, we don't have time to. . . ."

Suddenly, they heard grunts, curses, and the pounding of boots on the sidewalk just outside the office. It was too late to escape.

"Damn!" Joe hissed, racing over to find his gun and tomahawk. "Ellen, get under the desk and hide!"

There was no time to argue. Ellen dived under the desk just as Olsen kicked his door wide open, dragging inside both of the drunken fighters, one collared in each hand. He was struggling, and so intent on getting the drunks locked up in his jail that he didn't see Joe's attack from the side. Didn't see Joe's tomahawk as it swept a tight arc downward so that the thick flat of the blade smashed against his skull.

The sheriff collapsed beside the two struggling drunks. One of them looked up at Joe and saw the tomahawk. He opened his mouth to scream in terror, but Joe brought the flat side of the tomahawk down against his skull. The second drunk turned and tried his damnedest to crawl back outside, but Joe smashed him in the back of the head and he flopped and quivered.

"Joe!" Ellen cried. "You *killed* them!"

"Nope," he said. "I just used the flat of the blade on all three. Help me drag these two fools into the jail cell."

"What about the sheriff?" Ellen's heart was pounding wildly and she couldn't believe how fast and hard Joe had struck the three men. She was sure that at least one of them would never wake up and that she had witnessed at least one murder.

"Oh, Joe!"

"Just keep your nerve and hold steady, Ellen," Joe said in a voice that was amazingly calm and collected.

Ellen watched as Joe searched the office, pulling out all the desk drawers looking for his big roll of bills. He didn't find them in the desk, but he did find them cleverly hidden in one of the sheriff's ammunition boxes. And then Joe went over to Sheriff Olsen, and he dropped down on the man's back, sending a whoosh of air from the lawman's lungs.

"You thievin', rotten, badge-totin' sonofabitch," Joe said, drawing his bowie knife. "All you got now is a nice head of hair, and by gawd I'm gonna take even that!"

Ellen threw herself at Joe just as he was about to scalp the corrupt lawman and leave him on the floor to die. "No, please, Joe! I'm begging you not to do this."

"But he *deserves* it. Who knows how many other men Olsen has arrested and robbed and then let a mob hang to cover up his own crimes? And they *were* going to hang me, Ellen. It would have happened tomorrow morning . . . tomorrow night at the latest. Olsen would have let 'em hang

153

me so he could keep my money, my horse, and my new hat and boots! He even bragged about it this evening."

It was all happening so fast that Ellen felt dizzy. "Please, Joe. I've lost most everything by coming here to help you. If you kill Olsen, then I'll know that I've done the wrong thing. But if you let Sheriff Olsen live and just leave with me right now . . . then, then . . . I'll have no regrets no matter what happens to me."

Joe seemed to hang in dubious suspension as he weighed what had been said both by Ellen Johnson and Sheriff Olsen.

"Please, Joe."

"Oh, all right, dammit!" he growled, grabbing Olsen by his right ear and slicing it off close to the head. The unconscious man groaned and slapped at the blood, but he didn't awaken.

Ellen gasped and almost fainted at the sight of the ear, which Joe threw into the cell with disgust.

Joe lifted her up. "Olsen won't die, but he'll be marked as a thief for life and remember his wicked ways every time he looks at himself in the mirror."

"And he'll hate you with his dying breath," Ellen said, knowing it was true.

"A lot of men have hated me and a lot of

men have died," Joe said, pocketing his roll of money.

He then dragged Olsen into the cell along with the two unconscious drunks. Joe chuckled to himself as he locked the heavy cell door and shoved the key ring down beside his greenbacks.

"Let's get out of this town," he said to Ellen. "Let's get out of Carson City and never come back here again."

Ellen was so shocked by his casualness and sudden good spirits that it was all she could do to nod her head.

So they slipped out of the office and ducked down an alley. Staying in the darkest shadows where she could see nothing, but where Joe Moss seemed to have the eyes of a cat, they soon worked their way to behind the livery barn.

"Where are we going next?" she asked.

"To find Fiona," he said, mounting his horse bareback.

"But, Joe, I don't want to go up there! It's said to be a sinful place. As for your Fiona . . . I. . . ."

Joe dismounted and bent to kiss her on the forehead. "Now will you tell me what happened to your pretty face?" he asked, his good spirits suddenly gone.

"Eli Purvis backhanded me off his wagon

on the way home to Genoa this afternoon," she said. "But it's nothing, really."

Joe's face hardened like a tombstone in the graveyard moonlight. "Purvis did that, huh? And I bet he's planning to drive you from your farm and take it from you for no payment."

"Joe, please, it's all right."

"No, it ain't!" Joe said loud enough to cause a dog to bark from nearby. "Dammit, Ellen, I'm tired of people robbin' people and thinkin' they can get away with it."

"But it's my place and I've taken what's most important. Joe, we just have to —"

"We have to pay Eli Purvis a visit and see how much he's going to pay you for your farm, Mrs. Johnson. That's what we have to do."

For the briefest of moments, Ellen started to argue. But then she thought, *Joe Moss is honestly right! It is my farm and I deserve to be paid for it. My late husband and I settled that farm and we gave blood, sweat, and tears to make it a good and profitable farm.*

"All right, Joe. We'll go pay Mr. Purvis a visit and see if he wants to buy my farm."

"Oh, he'll buy it all right." Joe helped her onto her horse. "He'll buy it for a fair price, too, or my name ain't 'Man Killer' Joe Moss."

Hearing this, Ellen shivered slightly, although it might have been because of a sudden chill breeze sweeping down from the Sierras. But then she reined her horse around and they rode out of Carson City, heading for something that Ellen knew had been destined to happen since the moment her dear husband had passed.

15

Ellen Johnson should have been exhausted. After all, she'd walked a good ten miles back to her farm after being backhanded off a wagon seat. She was in pain and hadn't slept a wink the entire night . . . but she had never felt so alive . . . or so sure that she was in the right and about to be set free. Where that freedom would lead her, she had no idea. Joe Moss was in love with a memory that might or might not become a reality. Ellen couldn't count on Joe, but she knew now that she could always count on herself. She had acted with courage to free Joe and save him from a hangman's noose that he did not deserve. Now she would forever cut the ties between herself and this Mormon settlement.

After that, she would just have to pray and hope for the best.

Joe reined up the Palouse horse when they came to Ellen's farm. He stood up in his stirrups and stretched his long, lean frame and studied the farm. "You turned loose all your farm animals," he said more to himself than to her.

"Yes. I set everything free last night. Including you, Joe. I pray that I did the right thing and that God will judge me favorably."

"He will, but Eli Purvis and his bunch won't." Joe bent forward in his saddle and studied the Purvis farm intently. "Ellen, I want you to go back to your house and wait for me."

But she shook her head. "I can't do that."

"It'd be better for me and for Purvis if you weren't there."

"I have something to say to him, Joe. He struck me down and told me that I was going to lose everything since I refused to marry him. Now . . . now I judge it is my turn to tell Purvis a thing or two."

Joe pondered on that for a moment, lightly tapping the horn of his saddle. "All right," he agreed, "but if Purvis goes for a gun and tries to kill me, I'll have to defend myself. And when I kill him, you'll be considered by everyone to be a part of that. Is that okay with you, Ellen? Because if it isn't, you'd best go home for a while."

"I want your word that you will not kill him except in self-defense. Eli has three wives and twelve children. They're *good* children. I used to be their teacher so I know the oldest ones very well, and they would suffer terrible grief and hardship if they lost their father."

"All right. I won't kill Purvis unless I have to."

"Your word on it?"

A slow grin crossed his rugged and battered face. "Yeah, Ellen. You got Joe Moss's word on it. I won't kill him unless he tries to kill me first."

"Fair enough," she said. "Let's go settle up with the man."

As they rode toward the Purvis farmhouse with the first light of day streaking across the eastern sky, they could see a light in the window and smoke curling lazily from the chimney. The three Purvis wives would already be up and preparing breakfast. Purvis himself would probably be out in his big log barn milking or feeding his cows.

"Ellen, I need to know something right now."

"What?"

"How much is your farm worth?"

Ellen's attention was so focused on the Purvis cabin that she had to ask Joe to repeat his question, which he did "It's hard to say because no one but Mormons are allowed to own land in this little valley. These people only buy and sell to each other."

"You've got to give me a fair dollar value," Joe insisted. "For the house, the land, for all of it."

"Two thousand would be fair," she said after long deliberation. "But that would include my wagons, equipment, and the hay crop coming up in the fields."

"Two thousand." Joe clucked his tongue. "That sounds kinda low to me, but I'll take your word on it. Will Eli Purvis have that much money?"

"I don't know. The Mormons in this settlement don't trust the Carson City banks. The elders urge everyone to keep their money well hidden. I'm sure that Eli has hidden his cash. My guess would be in his barn."

"It's not going to stay hidden for long," Joe vowed, reining the Palouse up the two ruts in the road leading to the Purvis farmhouse.

Ellen didn't know what to do or think. Before she had made it clear she would never consent to marry Eli, she had been good friends with these people, especially Eli's wives, who were devoted, extremely hardworking, and always kind.

"Eli is doing chores in his barn just as I

figured," Ellen said, raising a hand and pointing. "See the light coming through the crack of the door?"

"I see it," Joe said, altering the direction of his horse with the slightest touch of rein. "You want to say good-bye to the man's wives and children?"

"What could I possibly say to them?"

"Good-bye," Joe said. "That's enough, I reckon."

"*Don't* kill him, Joe."

"I won't," he said over his shoulder. "If I killed him, he couldn't tell us where he hid all his money, now could he?"

If that remark was meant to be a joke, Ellen thought it an awfully poor one as she rode up to the front of the log house and dismounted.

Joe Moss reined up in front of the barn and tied the Palouse to a broken-down wagon. He now had a gun on his hip along with the tomahawk and bowie knife. For months and months he had been aware of the intense pressure that Eli Purvis had placed upon Ellen. And of the subtle threats he had made and the not-so-subtle references he had offered as to her relationship with the outsider, Joe Moss. And all that time Joe had kept quiet, knowing he would leave this valley and sure that Ellen Johnson would probably stay and wed a better Mormon farmer and maybe even find happiness again as a member of this tightly closed religious and farming community.

Joe had accepted that outcome. He was going to find and marry Fiona and reclaim the child he had fathered, yet had never seen. Yeah, Joe had bit his tongue and kept silent, even when Eli Purvis made cutting, hurtful remarks in his presence that he knew had deeply wounded Ellen Johnson.

But now that was all in the past. The man had made his play and he had shown his true colors when he'd slapped Ellen so hard he'd smashed her lips and hurt her in a fall from his wagon. Then, on top of everything, he'd left her to limp home like some stray dog.

"Well, Mr. Purvis, there always comes a day of reckoning and I reckon this is your day," Joe said as he pushed open the crack in the barn door and marched inside.

Eli was astraddle a three-legged stool milking a Jersey cow. His broad shoulders were hunched low under the animal's soft and ponderous belly, and his strong hands were sending long squirts of warm milk into a pail. Every squirt struck the side of the pail with a sharp, tinny ring that was as steady as the beat of a metronome.

The cow and a flock of chickens saw Joe first. The cow just stared at him as he approached, its large, vacuous brown eyes steady as it contentedly chewed its cud. A huge red rooster squawked and flew up into the hayloft, deserting his flock of hens. Eli Purvis was the only living thing in that barn unaware of Joe Moss, until his stool was suddenly kicked out from under him.

Eli tumbled backward, spilling the pail of milk across the dirt and straw. The cow just looked closer at Joe and then continued to chew its cud.

"What the. . . ."

Joe smiled, but it wasn't a smile that warmed the heart. Rather, it was a smile that froze the blood and chilled to the bone. "Eli," he said, "you struck Mrs. Johnson in the mouth, knocking her clear off your wagon. Then you didn't even have the decency to apologize and help her back into her seat. For that, I'm going to beat the living shit out of you right now."

Eli wasn't as tall as Joe, but he was the same age and heavier. His hand reached out, and he tried to right the pail and recover some of the milk. Then, without a word, he rolled and swung the pail straight at Joe's face.

The throw was hard and it connected. Milk splashed across Joe's eyes, momentarily blinding him. By the time he managed to scrub some vision back into his watery eyes, Eli Purvis was grabbing a pitchfork and charging Joe like a bull with four sharp and deadly horns. Only, these were steel tines and they hummed with deadly intent.

Joe was suddenly on the defensive and there wasn't time to draw one of his weapons, so he retreated until his back slammed up against a big post supporting the loft. He jumped behind the heavy pine post, and the pitchfork's tines bit into the wood with such force that they stuck.

Joe came back around the post with Eli swearing and trying to tear the pitchfork free. Joe could have drawn his knife and ripped open the farmer's belly, but he'd given a promise to Ellen and a promise to a lady had to be kept. So instead of gutting the farmer, Joe hit him in the center of the face with such force that Eli's head snapped back and his nose gushed like a crimson fountain.

But Eli Purvis wasn't ready to quit. Wiping blood from his face, he charged Joe again and this time, despite taking a hard left hand to the jaw, the farmer plowed in and grabbed Joe around the chest and began to crush him with a hold that forced all the breath out of Joe's lungs. And then Eli tossed Joe into another post, cracking the back of his skull hard.

For a moment, Joe felt all the strength go out of him. He was on his back now and Eli was on top hammering him with powerful blows. Joe kicked up with his long legs and locked his ankles across Eli's face. It was a move he'd done before when wrestling hard with mountain men and Indians. With a tremendous bellow of effort, Joe jerked Purvis over backward and shifted his hold so that it was under the farmer's chin. Ankles locked, legs straining with great power, Joe lay on his own back while he began to increase the pressure in what could have been a deadly stranglehold. In fact, he had seen one fighter choke his opponent to death with just such a hold.

But Joe had no intention of killing Eli Purvis; he just wanted to take the fight out of the farmer. So he held the ankle choke until Purvis turned purple in the face and stopped struggling. At the very last minute, before the man would have been asphyxiated, Joe released his ankle lock.

He crawled over to Purvis, watching the man struggle for air. Joe drew his bowie knife and grabbed Purvis by his beard saying, "Think I'm gonna shave it off, Eli. All you Genoa Mormons have long beards and I'm gonna make you stand out among the rest."

Terror filled the farmer's eyes as Joe dragged the sharp blade of his bowie knife down the man's cheek, cutting flesh along with whiskers. Purvis tried to shout and fight Joe off, but Joe kept at the man's face with his blade until it was hairless and badly lacerated.

"Now," Joe said, "I'm sure you heard about how much I like scalps. Well, Eli, I'm going to lift a patch of *your* scalp. I'll admit that there isn't much to lift, since you're pretty damned bald, but I'll take a patch off the back. That'll do me just fine 'cause I never been finicky."

"No, please, no!"

Joe sat astraddle the big farmer, keeping the man's hands and arms pinned under his legs. "I'm gonna scalp you, Eli, unless you give Mrs. Johnson two thousand dollars, which is fair pay for her good farm and everything on it."

"What?"

Joe didn't like to repeat himself, but he did because Purvis probably wasn't of a clear mind. "I said that I'm gonna scalp you

167

and then kill you if you don't buy her farm, which is worth at least two thousand dollars."

"I don't have two thousand dollars and I'm not. . . ."

Just for show, Joe dragged the big tomahawk from his belt and shoved one side of Eli's face into the dirt and spilled milk. "Now here's a decent patch of scalp. Take a deep breath, Eli, and try not to scare your kids by screamin' too loud."

"Okay!" he sobbed. "I'll buy her farm!"

"Cash," Joe said. "Right now."

"I don't have it here!"

Joe placed the sharp blade of his tomahawk against Eli's skull. "That's fine because I sure am sure going to enjoy taking your scalp."

"No! I'll pay!"

"Good. My guess is that you've hidden all your money right here in this barn."

It *was* a guess, but it turned out to be a good one. "Yes!" Purvis cried. "It's here."

Joe stood and allowed the farmer to crawl to his feet. Eli's crudely shaved face was awash in blood. He was trembling like an aspen leaf and unsteady. The cow was now starting to moan nervously, not sure why its udder wasn't being completely emptied.

Joe raised his tomahawk threateningly.

"Dig up your damned money, farmer!"

Eli staggered over to a place on the floor and collapsed to his knees with a frustrated sob. He dug like a badger and out came a big metal canister. As he fumbled to open it, Joe tore it from Eli's grasp and pried off the lid with a fingernail. He reached in and found a sizable wad of money.

"It's all the savings I have in this world!" Eli cried. "Think of my wife and family!"

"I am thinking of them, which is why I'm not going to kill you," Joe told the man. Then he carefully counted out two thousand dollars. Every last cent. "Looks like you got another hundred or so left," Joe announced.

"That's nothing if my crops fail or I lose livestock to sickness or —"

Joe silenced the man's whining. "Look at the bright side of this situation, farmer. I gave you a free shave. On top of that, you've got a couple hundred dollars in cash, three slaves that you call your wives, and all those fine, healthy children who will work for you when you grow old. On top of that, now you have *two* farms! Why, you're a very, wealthy and fortunate man!"

"Goddamn you!" Eli cried, lunging for the last of his money.

As he did so, Joe kicked him square in the balls. It was a vicious, hold-back-nothing kick that would guarantee that Eli did not father any more children for a long, long time. Maybe never.

Purvis went down howling. And he kept on howling until Ellen burst into the barn followed by the Purvis wives and some of the older children. One of the wives fainted and two of the children burst into tears.

"Did you kill him!" Ellen yelled accusingly at Joe.

"Nope, just made him a true believer."

"In *what?*"

Joe handed the two thousand dollars to Ellen. "In honest business dealings with his neighbors, of course. Ellen, Mr. Purvis just bought your farm for two thousand dollars. Didn't you, Eli?"

When Eli didn't answer, Joe stepped up to kick him again and make the farmer a true gelding. But then Eli cried out that, yes, he had bought the Johnson farm for two thousand dollars.

"Ellen," Joe said, "do you need a bill of sale?"

"No," she said in a tight voice, "these women are honest. They're all witnesses."

Joe sheathed his bowie knife and belted his tomahawk. "Then I do believe that our business is finished here."

"Not quite," Ellen said, her face grim as

she approached the writhing man on the ground. Through her swollen and blood-crusted lips, she hissed, "Eli, you slandered my name, you turned all the people against me when I did a Christian act for Joe, and . . . finally . . . you struck me hard in the face without feeling, remorse, or just cause."

And then . . . to Joe's complete amazement . . . Ellen Johnson reared back and kicked Eli in the crotch so hard, her body came off the ground and the farmer roared in agony.

Ellen turned and faced the two standing Purvis wives. "I'm pretty sure you women won't have to service your husband for a long, long time. And for that, I'm sure you'll secretly thank me."

The women clutched each other tightly, and then pulled their children outside so that they could not see their terrified and mutilated father weeping and moaning in the dirt.

Up in the loft, the red rooster crowed and some of his hens flew up to keep him company. Joe almost laughed because it struck him that Eli Purvis wouldn't be mounting any of his hefty and obedient wives soon, but the big red rooster sure as hell would be.

16

Joe Moss and Ellen Johnson skirted Carson City on their journey up to the Comstock Lode. They followed the meandering Carson River eastward, then turned slightly north and picked up the well-traveled road that ran up Gold Canyon into the barren hills toward Mount Davidson. Even down low on the hills, Joe and Ellen saw hundreds of small mines where rough-looking men dug furiously into the side of the barren hills hoping to strike it rich. You could easily tell how far they'd progressed by the size of their mine tailings. And along the road, heavily traveled by ore and timber freighters, were signs posted every few hundred feet reminding travelers that they would be "shot on sight" if they so much as set foot on one of the claims.

Joe was amazed at all the miners, most of them living in little caves or even holes in the ground covered with brush and canvas.

As a mountain man he'd lived in some primitive conditions, but this beat anything for hard times that he'd seen yet. "Ellen, I wonder how well all these fellas are doin' working dry claims this far down from the Comstock Lode."

"From the looks of them," she said, "I'd say they weren't doing very well. They're all thin and down at the heels. They're poorer-looking than the Paiute Indians."

"That's why I think that they oughta dig up closer to Virginia City," Joe said with a sad shake of his head.

But a little later that day, when Joe asked a miner who was dressed in rags why he didn't go up to the Comstock Lode, where there was a greater chance to strike it rich, the man explained the way of things in short order.

"A common workingman like me can't begin to buy a claim up on the Comstock Lode. Why, the prices of claims up there go for hundreds of dollars a running foot!"

"Are you serious?" Joe asked with astonishment.

"Of course I am!" the ragged miner snapped. "Why else would all of us be diggin' in these dry hills so far from the lode? And besides that, all the real gold and silver is too deep to reach by tunneling. You see, it's buried far underground in big pockets."

"Then how do they reach it?" Ellen asked.

The miner spat a chew of tobacco and shook his head. "Shoot, you two don't know nothin', do you?"

"No," Joe admitted. "I was a trapper, then a wagon train master, and finally a freighter. I've never been a miner and don't intend to become one."

"You're smart," the prospector said with a look of dejection. "You got any tobacco I can smoke or chew?"

Joe gave the man his pouch and papers. The miner nodded his appreciation and rolled a cigarette. He lit it and inhaled deeply. "Damn, that tastes good," he sighed as the smoke curled out of his nostrils. He gazed eastward toward barren hills that stretched on forever. "Gawd, but I hate this country."

"Then why don't you leave it?"

The man inhaled deeply again and shook his head. "Because this Comstock Lode is the richest and biggest strike I'll ever see in my lifetime."

"Even bigger than the one in California?" Joe asked.

"It's too early to say, but I think it will be. The difference is that in California the little man could get lucky and strike it rich if he found a few big nuggets. Not here, though. People like me are just scratchin' the belly of this mountain and barely makin' bean and flour money."

"Maybe you should take up another line of work," Joe said.

"I can't. All I know is how to dig for gold and silver."

Joe frowned. "Mister, it sounds to me like you're playin' a losin' game down here in this gulch."

"I am," the prospector admitted. "But I've got gold fever just as bad as I did ten years ago on the other side of the Sierras. Trouble is, us Forty-Niners who panned out the cold rivers runnin' off the western slopes of the Sierras came here and were told that we had to go deep down in cages and learn all about hard-rock mining."

"What do you mean *cages?*" Ellen asked.

"It's like this, ma'am. All the mining up on the Comstock Lode is done with hydraulics and it's the big companies that are hirin' miners. No one mines for themselves up there because they ain't got the money to buy all the heavy machinery it takes to go underground hundreds of feet. But the big mine companies have done it and they run twenty-four-hour shifts. They drop their miners down in cages lowered on twisted wire cables. Drop 'em hundreds of feet into the belly of the mountain, and bring 'em up the same way after twelve-hour shifts in hell."

Joe shook his head. "I don't think I'd ever go down on a cage that deep. Do the cables ever break?"

"All the damned time," said the miner bitterly. "And when those wire cables snap, the miners can kiss their . . . well, ma'am, I guess you can imagine what it would be like droppin' a couple of hundred or even a thousand feet down a dark hole. They say there isn't much left you can recognize of a man who falls that far to the bottom."

Ellen Johnson looked a little pale. "I'd imagine not."

"What happened to your faces?" the prospector said, eyes shifting from Joe to Ellen and back again. "No offense, but did you two whip up on each other?"

"No," Ellen said, smiling a little even though it hurt her lips. "We're the very best of friends."

"Well," the prospector said, drawing hard on his cigarette so that it burned down to his fingers, "you need to stick together up there in Virginia City. There are more thieves and murderers up there than you can imagine, and all they live for is to skin you alive after takin' every last cent of your money."

"Thanks for the warning," Joe said. "Have you found any gold yet?"

"Barely enough to keep me in bread and beans."

"Have you thought about going to work for the big Comstock Lode mines?" Ellen asked him.

"Oh, I think about it most all the time I'm awake, ma'am. They have a miners union up in Virginia City, and those fellas that go down in the deep mines earn four dollars a day. Can you imagine that! Why, four dollars a day is the highest miner's wages in the world. They got fellas comin' from the hard-rock mines in England, Ireland, and Wales. There are hundreds of men just itchin' for jobs at the big mines like the Consolidated and the Bullion. But that ain't the life for me. I always worked for myself and I don't like being out of sight of God's pure sunshine."

"Amen," Joe said. "I don't know how men can work that deep underground."

"They do it strictly for the money," the prospector said, taking the last deep drag on his cigarette. "But the Virginia City and Gold Hill cemeteries there are fillin' up fast from all the mine accidents. Men fallin' outa those flimsy cages, or slammin' their picks through a wall holding back boilin' water and gettin' scalded to death. Havin' tunnels and shafts collapse on 'em so deep under the ground that nobody even bothers to try and find 'em for a Christian burial. No, sir! I don't care if they do earn four dollars a day. I just can't do it. They say that some men go crazy in that hot hell down under the mountain, and I'm afraid I'd do the same."

"Here," Joe said, tossing the man his tobacco pouch and papers. "I'll buy some more up in Virginia City."

"Thank you kindly," the prospector said. "I'll take your gift in exchange for the advice I freely gave you both. Last thing I'll say is that everything up there is higher than the moon. Those three fine horses of yours? They'll cost a small fortune to board because anything and everything in Virginia City has to be hauled over from Lake's Crossing, or even all the way from Sacramento and San Francisco. That's why they're payin' those poor bastards four dollars a day to work in their deep-rock mines."

Joe nodded with understanding and thanked the man for his time before they continued up the rocky road in Gold Canyon.

■ ■ ■ ■

Later that afternoon, the canyon narrowed and they came to a place where it pinched in so tight that two big wagons would have had trouble passing through side by side. There was a line of freight wagons backed up, and a man was taking money from everyone that passed through his narrow portal.

"What is going on here?" Ellen asked.

Joe scowled. "Looks to me like someone thinks he can charge everyone money who goes through that narrow pass. Damned if he'll charge us, though."

"Joe, if everyone else has to pay, then we probably will, too."

"The hell with that," Joe said, spurring his horse forward past the waiting wagons until he came to the toll taker. "What is goin' on here, mister!"

The man collecting money glared at Joe and snapped, "Get back in line and wait your turn to pay your fare so you can pass through Devil's Gate."

If there was one thing that riled Joe Moss, it was taking orders. "The hell I'll pay you!"

The man was big and rough-looking. He glanced at Joe, then pointed up to both sides of the pass where he had riflemen posted. "Oh, you'll pay," he said, " 'cause if you try to go through here without payin', then my boys will shoot you dead."

Joe studied the two riflemen up above. They had Winchester rifles and they looked like they knew how to use them. However, he had never paid a toll to anyone other than a ferryman who had to work hard to get him and his horse across a wide, swift river. This, however, was entirely different, and it stuck in his craw like sand.

"How do you get away with this bullshit?" Joe demanded.

"I own this piece of property called Devil's Gate and that gives me the right to charge everyone a toll. Now, if you don't like paying me a dollar each, then you can turn that horse around and ride about five miles back down this canyon and then another ten miles to start up the mountain from the north like the folks do from Lake's Crossing. It's called Six Mile Canyon, and it'll take you an extra day of hard riding."

Joe had no intention of losing a full day. "I ain't got that much extra time."

"Then ride that horse back to your place in line and wait your turn to pay. Those three horses you have will cost you three dollars."

"That's highway robbery!"

The man laughed, but it was not a nice sound. "I told you your choices. Now quit wastin' my time, mister."

Joe wanted to get off his horse and whip this sonofabitch who owned Devil's Gate and had riflemen posted ready and willing to kill for a lousy few dollars. But he was with Ellen and he wanted to make sure she got settled somewhere safe. Also, he was nearly to Virginia City and his beloved Fiona. Considering all that, he decided that he would swallow the sand sticking in his craw and pay the outrageous toll.

But if he ever caught this man in some saloon or by himself, he was going to kick his ass up between his bat ears and then mark his hide, by gawd!

After paying, he and Ellen continued up the canyon through the bustling little mining community called Gold Hill. They stopped at a little café and had something to eat that wasn't good and was very expensive.

"How much farther is it to Virginia City?" Ellen asked the café owner.

"About a mile and a half to The Divide that separates our two towns."

"That all?" Joe asked, feeling his heart beat a little faster with anticipation.

"Yep. But it's the steepest mile and a half you've ever seen wagons being hauled up. It's a corkscrew road and there are a lot of runaways between Gold Hill and Virginia City. And mister, if one of those big freight wagons breaks loose at the top of The Divide and comes barrelin' down that curve at you, it's the end."

Joe nodded with understanding. "We'll be watchin' for that," he said.

"See that you do. You have three horses?"

"Yep."

"It'll cost you a fortune to board 'em up in Virginia City. You could keep them in my corral for only a dollar a day."

"For all three?"

"Hell, no! A dollar *each* per day."

Joe almost fell over. "Mister," he said, "you've already scalped us for this sorry meal. Now you want to do the same to our horses? No, thanks."

The café owner laughed. "You'll see when you get up there what I'm talking about. Mostly, they're finding silver, and it assays at an honest $3,000 per ton! That's the richest ore that has ever been discovered in the West, so unless you've got a big fat wad of money, you and your horses will end up eating dirt by next week."

Joe started to grab the man and shake

some manners into him, but Ellen stepped in between saying, "Now, Joe, let's just get on up to Virginia City without any more trouble today. After all, Fiona and your child are up there and you've already waited too long to find them."

"Yeah," Joe said, "I guess you're right."

So he helped her out the door and then onto her horse. The sun struck her hair and it shone real pretty in the high desert sunlight. Ellen Johnson was, Joe thought, really quite a looker. And he was sure that she would soon have a line of admirers standing to win her hand and her heart.

Joe smiled. That was good and it was right. Ellen deserved the very best, but then so did Fiona McCarthy.

17

"Well," Joe said, his eyes drinking in the famed mining town of Virginia City, "there she be! The Queen of the Comstock Lode, just like that sign says."

Ellen studied the big sign at the top of the steep grade that told them they had indeed reached Virginia City, whose latest population numbered over two thousand. "See, Joe, aren't you glad that you can read?"

"I sure am," he said. "Look at the size of this place and all the building that's going on here! Why, I never seen anything like it before. Everything is built on the side of this steep old mountain."

Virginia City was teeming with business and activity. The main street leading into town was clogged with people, horses, and wagons. Everywhere you looked there were houses, shacks, and businesses being erected, and Joe could see at least half a dozen huge mines belching smoke into the clear blue sky. What was missing was the color green. There wasn't a pine or shade tree in sight nor a blade of green grass. Instead, the Comstock Lode was all rock and sage and soft brown dirt. Once there had been some scrubby piñon and juniper pines on the slopes of Mount Davidson, but they had long since been chopped down for firewood or timbering.

"What do you think, Ellen?"

"It's even worse than I'd imagined," she said. "I'm not sure that a Mormon farm girl like me can stand it up here for long. I don't even see so much as a flower or a tomato plant growing in anyone's yard."

"You don't have to stay," Joe told her with genuine concern. "We can sell your horses and put you on a stagecoach."

"But where would I go?" she asked. "I could never return to Genoa, and I certainly don't want to return to Carson City."

"You must have kinfolks someplace that would be happy to see you."

"I don't," she admitted. "They're back in Indiana and they are also of the Mormon faith. When they learn what I've done. . . ."

Her words trailed off, and Joe understood. "Look," he said, "I'm sure that there are some nice women up here that will help you feel at home."

"I wonder," she said. "But let's go find out about Fiona and your child, Joe. Their absence has been driving you for too long."

Joe tugged his hat down a little, feeling a sudden nervousness. "What if Fiona is married again?"

"I don't know what to tell you about that."

"Or maybe she's in love with someone else now."

"Joe, let's quit this worrying and find out."

"All right," he said, squaring his broad shoulders. "Let's do that, only. . . ."

"Only what?"

"Only how can we even start to find them here? There are so many people in Virginia City that it won't be easy."

But Ellen disagreed. "A young woman like your Fiona will turn heads and be remembered by everyone. And she'll have a child, which I expect will be very unusual in this wild mining town. And then there is her father. What did you say his name was?"

Joe spat into the dirt. "Brendan McCarthy, but he's no damned good."

"Doesn't matter," Ellen said. "If we find him, we'll find your Fiona and child. He's Fiona's father and he might be mean and petty, but he'll still know of his daughter."

"Yeah, I expect that's true enough. I was just hopin' never to have to lay my eyes on him again."

"Put the past behind you, Joe. That's what I've been telling myself ever since we left Carson City. We've both crossed the bridge where there is no turning back, so let's go find her and your child."

Joe set his Palouse horse into motion and rode up C Street into the heart of Virginia City. The downtown seemed like it was just one big saloon after another, and all of them were packed with miners, freighters, gamblers, and shills. Piano music poured into the street, and most of the people Joe saw appeared dead drunk.

"There's a newspaper office," Ellen said. "That would be a good place to start asking about Fiona and her father."

"It would?"

"Sure. Their business is to know other people's business."

Joe and Ellen tied their horses to a hitching rail in front of the office of the newspaper, the *Territorial Enterprise,* and entered the building, where typesetters were busy in the back of the large room filled with a gigantic printing press, while editors and reporters were buzzing around preparing copy.

"Can I help you?" a tall, good-looking man with angular features asked.

"I'm Joe Moss and this is Mrs. Johnson. We're looking for a woman named Fiona McCarthy."

The man smiled and raised his hands palms up. "I'm afraid we are not the Lost and Found. Maybe you should go to the sheriff's office."

"Sir," Ellen said, stepping forward, "it is a pleasure to meet you and I can see that you are very busy getting to press right now, so we won't waste your time. But Mr. Moss is searching for a young woman and his child . . . a child that he has never seen."

The newspaperman nodded with fresh interest. "Boy or girl?"

"I don't know yet," Joe said. "It's . . . it's a *complicated* story."

"And it sounds like a rather interesting one," the reporter said. "Perhaps worthy of being in our fine newspaper. Oh, my pen name is Dan DeQuille. And I'm sure you have heard of our famous reporter whose pen name . . . which is known far and wide . . . is none other than Mark Twain."

"Afraid I haven't heard of either of you," Joe confessed. "I only just learned to read and I'm not all that good at it yet."

DeQuille shrugged off his disappointment. "Well, would you like to give me some particulars on this missing person you're after? I won't promise you anything, but we might run your story in tomorrow's edition. And that way, if Fiona is still in Virginia City, she would certainly learn that you have come to claim her. You see, almost everyone in this town that can read does read the *Territorial Enterprise*."

Joe could see that the tall, handsome newspaperman was proud of both his profession and his paper. And the fella was probably correct. Fiona and her father were both readers, and would find out tomorrow that he was in town looking for them.

"Would it cost me to have you run the story?"

"Not one thin dime," DeQuille assured Joe. "Just you and your friend come back to my desk and tell me the story and I'll do my best to get it into print."

Since it cost nothing, Joe felt that this was a stroke of good fortune. With Ellen at his side, he told the newspaperman his story about falling in love with Fiona on a wagon train that he'd led west some years ago, and then how he'd lost her, but hoped to find her in the next day or two right here on the Comstock Lode.

"And you fathered this child out of wedlock?" DeQuille said in a quiet voice, not looking directly at Joe.

"I . . . yes, sir."

"Hmmm," DeQuille said, laying his ink pen down for a moment and folding his long, slender fingers together. "We'll have to be a bit careful about the child part. We don't want to embarrass Miss McCarthy. Also, you have to be prepared for the idea that she might have remarried. So as you can well understand, Mr. Moss, this is a *delicate* issue."

"All right," Joe said, "leave out the kid."

"I think that would be my preference," DeQuille told him as he finished asking a few more questions about Joe and Fiona. "Now," he said, "I think I have enough to compose the story. All our readers enjoy a good love story and that is what you have here, Mr. Moss."

"Joe. Just call me Joe."

"Very well," DeQuille agreed. "Now, Miss Johnson, I have to say that your story also interests me greatly. Where, exactly, did you come from and why did you leave your husband?"

DeQuille was very handsome in an elegant and erudite way. Not at all like a farmer or workingman. He had long, black hair slicked straight back over his skull and perfectly parted down the middle, along with large brown eyes. His hands were the most delicate that Joe Moss had ever seen on a man, and yet there was strength and great intelligence in his person, Joe was sure of it.

Ellen felt that, too. She realized at once that she was dealing with a man who had unusual charm and a gift for extracting the most personal and private information to write about. And because of that, she was on her guard.

"Mr. DeQuille," she said, "I am not here in your newspaper office to find anyone, nor do I want someone in my past to find me."

"How mysterious," DeQuille said with a wide grin. "It makes me even more determined to hear your story."

"I'm afraid that it is far too personal," Ellen told him firmly.

"Where will you both be staying?"

"We have no idea. Can you recommend lodging?"

DeQuille steepled his long fingers and thought a moment "I do know someone who runs a boardinghouse for ladies. It's up on B Street and I'll write you a note of introduction, if you wish."

"That would be extremely kind," Ellen said, visibly relieved. "And what about Joe?"

"What about Joe?" DeQuille asked, turning to him. "You can find boardinghouses all over town. There are a few hotels as well, some good and some little more than shacks. So it all depends on what you can afford."

"I have money," Joe told him. "I don't need anything fancy, but I won't sleep among thieves and drunks."

"Then you might want to board where I do," DeQuille said. "There is a small room that has just been vacated."

"Been what?"

"It is available for occupancy," DeQuille explained.

"How much?"

"Two dollars a day. Ten dollars a week. Thirty-five dollars a month."

"Holy cow!" Joe swore. "That's terrible high."

"Not for up here, Mr. Moss. I promise you it is a good bargain and it comes with hot water for a bath as well as a good breakfast. Dinner and supper are not included, however."

"I dunno," Joe hesitated. "Maybe I'll see if I can sleep in a stable by my horses and earn my keep by pitchin' hay and cleaning stalls."

"I'm afraid that you won't have any success at that," DeQuille explained. "Those kinds of jobs have a line of hungry and unemployed men waiting to fill them. Anyway, if you find your Fiona, perhaps she has accommodations more to your liking."

Joe blushed a little. "Yeah. I hope so."

Ellen said, "Joe, why don't you take the room for at least tonight? Tomorrow we'll know a lot more. But tonight we both could use a good, safe room and a bath."

"All right," Joe agreed. "But as soon as I find a place for our horses I'm going to go looking for her, and I won't stop until she's found."

"Good luck," DeQuille said, not sounding hopeful.

Once they were back outside the *Territorial Enterprise,* Joe took the three horses and went to find them a stable, while Ellen took off for the boardinghouse that Mr. DeQuille had recommended and had also graciously given her a note of introduction for.

Joe rode his Palouse horse and led Ellen's horses up the street and, not finding a stable, he began to search on higher and lower streets until he found a stable that looked well run. However, when he asked about the price, he was nearly dumbfounded to learn that it was going to cost him twenty-one dollars a week for the three animals, more if he wanted them grained.

"I swear that's higher'n a camel's back!"

"That may be so," the liveryman agreed with a smile, "but all the hay and grain have to be brought clear over from the Carson Valley. The freight alone cost me a fortune. Now, if you want to sell those horses, you could save yourself a lot of money."

"No, thanks," Joe said. "A man without a horse is only half a man."

The livery owner laughed. "My sentiments exactly! Now, I expect payment in advance."

Joe paid the man and departed the stable with his money, saddlebags, and weapons. His heart began to race as he headed back down to C Street just hoping that he would bump into Fiona among the crowds. Yet, he knew in his heart that he would not because it quickly became apparent that the only women on the street were whores trying to entice men into cheap hotel rooms and back-alley cribs.

Joe turned them all down, although he sure was yearning for the soft, enticing flesh of a woman. But Fiona was real close now. He could almost feel her presence, and he'd be damned if he'd soil his body and soul just before seeing her again. So he smiled at the aggressive whores and turned his back on them as he walked the sidewalks packed with humanity.

Then, right out of the blue . . . just like a

nightmare . . . he collided with the drunken wreckage and dissipation of Brendan Mc-Carthy.

18

Joe Moss and Brendan McCarthy were about the same height, but that was where their similarities ended. Now, standing face-to-face with the man that he hated as much as any before in his life, Joe found himself stunned and completely at a loss for words.

"You," Brendan muttered, his bloodshot eyes dilating with abhorrence. "You!"

And to Joe's great surprise, Fiona's drunken, worthless father lunged forward and grabbed Joe by the throat screaming, "I'll kill you!"

Joe felt the man's thumbs digging into his neck and spine. Despite his advancing age and poor health, Brendan was still amazingly powerful. Joe threw his arms up, and it was a struggle to break the old man's death grip. They tripped, fell off the sidewalk into the street, and Brendan landed on top of Joe.

For an instant, Joe's right hand shot down

to his bowie knife and grabbed its handle. Had he not been sober and in full control of his senses, Joe would have drawn the knife and plunged it deep under Brendan McCarthy's rib cage. He would have killed this old bastard in the blink of an eye . . . but now he could not because this man was still Fiona's beloved father.

So instead of knifing the drunken Irishman, Joe drew his six-gun and slammed it up against the side of Brendan's thick skull. It took three powerful blows before Brendan's eyes crossed and he toppled over unconscious.

"Did you *kill* that old Irish sot?" another drunk asked, lurching off the sidewalk to stand over Joe and Brendan. "I hope you killed him because he ain't worth the air that he breathes. And he's mean as a rattlesnake and about as trustworthy as a rabid skunk."

Joe staggered to his feet, using a horse-watering trough to support himself. His neck felt as if it had been snapped and his head was spinning. Batting the drunk aside with his gun, he plunged his head into the water trough and held it underwater for a full minute before he dragged himself erect and shook the water off his head.

"Shoot him!" the drunk urged. "Shoot

that ornery bastard while he's down and he'll never know what hit him. Be a real mercy to put him out of his misery and send him to the Promised Land . . . although he'll probably go straight to Hell instead."

Joe holstered his gun and used his sleeve to wipe his eyes. Vision restored and his head slowing down, he glared at the blood-thirsty man. "Do you know this man well?"

"Sure! Every drunk on C Street knows Brendan McCarthy to be nothing more than a low-down, lyin' sonofabitch."

"It's his daughter that I'm lookin' for to-day."

"She's gone. That's why McCarthy is always drunk."

Joe looked down at the unconscious Irish-man, then back at the one who'd been urging him to shoot Brendan. "McCarthy was always about half-drunk."

"Well, mister, he's now half-drunk al-ways." The miner cackled, pleased with his turn of words.

Joe shook his head. "Where's his daughter?"

The man gave Joe a loose and lopsided grin. "She may be dead."

Joe's heart nearly stopped. He jumped forward and grabbed the man by his shirt-front, growling, "Mister, if you're tryin' to be amusin', you're headin' in the wrong direction. Now tell me true where Fiona McCarthy is or I'll bust your head wide open and take your damned scalp!"

To make sure that the miner understood the seriousness of the situation, Joe drew his fearsome-looking tomahawk and raised it high.

"Oh, Sweet Jesus, don't kill me!"

"Where is Fiona McCarthy, damn you?" Joe roared.

"That ain't his daughter's name anymore, mister!"

Joe lowered his tomahawk, remembering that Fiona had been forced by her father to marry a man in California for his gold rush claim. "Then what *is* her name?"

"Brendan's daughter, if that's who you're huntin', goes by the name of Mrs. Fiona Moss."

"Huh?" Joe dropped the tomahawk. "What are you talkin' about? *My* last name is Moss."

The drunk tried to turn and run, but Joe was on him like a bird on a fat grub. He grabbed the miner and spun him around. Then, inspired by the effect that a good dunking had had on his own mental clarity, Joe shoved the drunk's head into the water trough and held it under counting to twenty-five.

"You're gonna drown him," a man said, looking very worried. "If you drown him, then you'll hang, mister."

"I ain't gonna drown him," Joe answered, finally letting the drunk up for air. "I'm just putting the fear of God upon him."

Joe threw the miner down in the dirt beside Brendan, and then he knelt between the two men. When the drunk stopped choking and heaving, Joe slapped him a couple of times hard and said, "Now where is his daughter?"

"I don't know!" the Comstock miner cried. "Honest, I don't! Old Brendan probably don't know, either! Only thing we know is that she disappeared more than a month ago."

Joe sagged with disappointment.

"Why don't you let me go, mister? I didn't do anything to you. He probably knows where she's hiding!"

Joe sat up and shook his head, as if that simple act could sort out all the clutter and make things sensible. But it didn't do anything. "All right," he said, "you go. I'll get my answers from Fiona's old man."

Joe grabbed Brendan's ankles and dragged the besotted Irishman out of the street before some freight wagon came along and cut him to pieces. He had attracted considerable attention from the mostly drunken miners who had little to do but look forward to their next hellish shift. But they had seen Joe raise that tomahawk, and not a one of them was of a mind to interfere.

When Joe got Brendan in between two buildings, he shook Fiona's father until the man finally regained consciousness. When he saw Joe, he tried to knock his head off, but Joe got on top of the Irishman and pinned his arms. Glaring down at Brendan, he shouted, "McCarthy, what the hell is the matter with you! Have you gone completely off your rocker from drinkin'?"

Brendan struggled some more, but he was tiring and finally stopped. "Get off me, Moss."

"If I do, are you goin' to go crazy again?" Joe really wanted to impress the old man, so he drew his knife. "If you are, then I might as well cut your worthless throat and be done with it. Something I should have done before I left that wagon train."

Brendan's eyes were red and watery. He had a beard that was about a week old and he stank worse than a pig. "Go ahead," the man challenged. "Cut my throat. It'd be a blessing to me and I'd go to hell knowin' you'd hang." Brendan began to half-laugh and half-cry. "I wouldn't take bets which one of us would burn the longer in hell!"

Joe could see that McCarthy was too far gone to be a threat and that the man really didn't care whether he lived or died. "Where is Fiona?" he asked. "I don't care about you. Only thing I care about is Fiona and my child."

"You mean your *bastard* daughter!"

Something snapped in Joe's mind and he clenched his left hand and brought it down into McCarthy's ruined and hateful face as if it were a sledgehammer. Brendan grunted and lost consciousness. His mouth hung open, and Joe could see that he had knocked out the old man's last remaining front teeth.

Joe stood up feeling a wave of disgust wash over him. "What am I doin'?" he asked. "Almost killin' a man that is already more dead than alive?"

Feeling weary, defeated, and a little sick to his stomach, Joe left the dim space between the buildings and dunked his head again in the water trough. Then he squared his shoulders, slapped the dirt and dust from himself, and tried to think of what to do next.

"Joe!"

It was Ellen and she was rushing up the boardwalk. When she stopped before him, she blurted out, "What on earth has happened to you?"

Joe didn't want to talk about it but he had to. In a few mumbled words he told her about bumping into Fiona's father and then being attacked by the old man. He ended up saying, "Fiona is gone. I got a . . . a daughter . . . somewhere."

"A daughter?" She smiled. "Joe, that's *wonderful* news!"

But it didn't feel to Joe even a little bit like wonderful news. "Fiona's father is lyin' there between the buildings. I hit him pretty hard. I'm kinda ashamed of myself for doin' it."

"Joe, you've really got me confused. Let's see to him and find out what is going on."

"All right," Joe said, "but I got a sudden real bad feeling in my gut. I'm not sure that I want to know what that old man can tell me about Fiona."

Ellen Johnson gave him a strange look that turned to sadness. "Joe," she said, taking him by the arm and leading him into the narrow space between the buildings where a dark and terrible truth was to be revealed, "let's just get Fiona's father and find out what happened to her and your daughter."

"Okay," he whispered, suddenly, and for

the first time in his long, difficult life, almost afraid.

19

"My god, Joe, I think you almost killed Mr. McCarthy! He's having a lot of trouble just breathing!"

They were crouched over the old Irishman in the dim corridor between two rough-sided board buildings. "Joe, we've got to find him a doctor!"

"I swear that he was fighting mad just a little while ago," Joe said, grabbing Brendan McCarthy's arms and dragging him out onto the boardwalk, where Joe could see that the Irishman was desperately struggling for air. Even worse was that the man's battered face was ashen and pasty-looking.

"Don't you dare die on me!" Joe shouted, kneeling over McCarthy. "You've got to tell me where Fiona is, *then* you can die!"

"Joe," Ellen commanded. "Go find a doctor. Hurry!"

"But there might not even be one up here on the Comstock."

"Try, Joe! You have to try and find help for Mr. McCarthy or his death will be on your hands."

Joe jumped to his feet and began to run down the boardwalk shouting. "Doctor! We need a doctor!"

Miners with drinks and bottles in their hands just shrugged with indifference, but were wise enough to step aside as Joe barreled past. Finally, a woman in her mid-fifties came forward to block Joe's path. "Dr. Taylor is just up the street a few doors."

"Which building?"

"That one," the woman said, pointing. "But there are nuns down at St. Mary of the Mountain Catholic Church that are better and will tend to the sick and dying for free."

"How far is that church where the nuns are to be found?"

"Way down the hill," the lady told him. "It's quite a long ways on foot, I'm afraid."

"No time for it," Joe told her, eyes searching for Dr. Taylor's office sign.

"Ma'am, I can read words good, but not names. Take me to Taylor 'cause a man is dyin' back there on the sidewalk."

The woman was decisive. She pulled up her skirts and took off in something like a rolling shamble, leading Joe to the doctor's little office. "Thank you, ma'am!"

Joe went inside to see three miners sitting in wooden chairs and a smallish man with a monocle in one eye examining a fourth miner's obviously broken arm. "Doc!" Joe cried. "I got a man just down the street who can't hardly breathe!"

Dr. Taylor turned from his patient and said, "Bring him on here and I'll have a look at him."

"But you don't understand, this fella is *dyin'*."

"Then go to the mortuary two doors down. They'll make all the funeral arrangements."

Joe rushed across the crowded little office, grabbed Taylor by the seat of his baggy pants with one hand and his coat collar with the other. He propelled the doctor across his waiting room and toward the door.

"Wait!" the doctor cried. "If you insist, at least let me take my medical bag!"

"All right, but you better hurry!"

They rushed outside and back to Ellen and Brendan McCarthy, who was still fighting for air and shaking badly.

Dr. Taylor looked to Ellen. "What happened to his face?"

"I punched him 'cause he was trying to strangle me," Joe confessed. "But I didn't hit him in the throat."

"He's got a high fever and his heart may be giving out," the doctor pronounced after making a quick examination.

"What can you do about that?"

"Nothing for the heart," the doctor replied. "By the looks of him, he's used himself badly in life. It may be his time."

Joe was so frustrated he could have screamed. Instead, he said in an almost pleading voice, "Doc, you gotta try and keep him alive long enough to tell me where to find his daughter and my daughter."

"What?" Dr. Taylor was confused.

"I need to talk to him! Ask him a few questions before he croaks."

Dr. Taylor looked to Ellen with pity. "Ma'am, you seem like the only one with any sense here besides myself. We need to get this man to my office as quickly as possible."

"Joe, pick him up!" Ellen ordered.

Joe was so desperate to learn where to find his Fiona that he scooped Brendan McCarthy up in his arms and started running back toward the doctor's office. Ellen and Taylor overtook him at the door, and they rushed the gasping Irishman into a back office where there was a stout wooden examination and operating table, dark-colored with the stain of blood.

"Lay him down and then leave," Dr. Taylor told them.

"But, Doc, I need to get some answers from him!"

"Get the hell out of this room!" Dr. Taylor bellowed.

"Come on," Ellen said, pulling Joe outside into the reception room, where the miner with the broken arm was gritting his teeth in agony.

One of the miners looked Joe up and down and then spat tobacco on the floor, showing his dislike. "It wasn't your turn to see the doc. Was our friend George's turn."

Joe's hand dropped to his tomahawk and he hissed, "Mister, it'll be *all* your turns with me and God if you don't shut your yaps!"

The four miners shut their yaps.

The next hour was one of the longest Joe had ever spent in his life. He'd demanded that the miners give up two chairs for Ellen and himself, and they'd only grudgingly done so. Joe didn't know if Brendan McCarthy was still alive or not, and once, when he'd pushed open the door to take a look, he'd witnessed Dr. Taylor administering some kind of medicine to McCarthy, and then the physician had yelled at him to close the door.

"I don't think he's gonna make it," Joe lamented, resuming his seat beside Ellen Johnson.

"Even if he doesn't, we'll still find your Fiona," Ellen consoled. "But Joe, why did you have to hurt that old man so badly?"

"He went for my throat like a wolf," Joe explained, knowing it was a sorry excuse. "McCarthy wanted to kill me. Can you imagine? And I'm the one that should be killin' him. I don't understand it. I knew he never liked me, but I never deserved his hatred."

Ellen pursed her lips and whispered, "Mr. McCarthy probably hates you for what you did to his daughter. Did you take her . . . her maidenhood?"

Joe flushed with humiliation. He couldn't speak for his shame and embarrassment. The best he could do was to nod his head that he had indeed deflowered little Fiona.

"Well, there you have it," Ellen said, laying a gentle hand on Joe's knee. "I know that you two were in love, but . . . well, you must understand what a father would feel like in Mr. McCarthy's circumstances."

"I guess I do," Joe admitted. He took a deep, shuddering breath. "Ellen, there was a man told me that Fiona has a daughter.

And besides that, Fiona McCarthy now calls herself Fiona Moss."

Tears put a sudden shine into Ellen's eyes. "That means that Fiona still loves you, Joe. That's the only thing that it could mean . . . her taking your last name for herself."

"Yeah," he said, nodding his big, stupid head. "I guess it does at that. But what about that little girl? She'd be . . . four years old . . . this month." Joe suddenly felt very low and his voice thickened with emotion. "Four years old and she's never even seen her real father."

"That may be about to change, Joe. Fiona and your little girl might still be in town. Don't give up so easy."

"I never do anything easy," he told Ellen. "But finding Fiona is about the hardest thing I ever tried."

"It's going to work out," Ellen promised, although she also had a bad feeling about the McCarthys.

"What's takin' so long in there?" the miner with the broken arm sobbed as he rocked back and forth in pain. "This arm is killin' me and it needs to be set and splinted. I need some powerful opium!"

"Maybe you should go look up a China-man," one of the miners suggested. "They'll sell it to you cheap enough."

"Aw, shut up!" the injured miner barked. "I got no money for opium. Not even for a bottle of whiskey. And how am I gonna feed myself if I can't work until this arm mends?"

"We'll all chip in for a while," one said after a long silence. "Won't we, boys?"

"That's right," another said as if trying to convince himself. "Wasn't George's fault that rotten timbers buckled and the roof dropped on him. Could have happened to any of us down there today. We'll talk to the head of the union first chance and raise some hell over that mine."

"Shit," another said with obvious disgust. "Our damned miners union isn't going to put up any fuss with the Consolidated Virginia Mine Company! Not on your life they won't. Why, the Consolidated has men begging to take our places standing fifty deep in line every shift."

"Well, they need to put in more timbering. Shore up those walls and ceilings!" another miner cried in helpless frustration. "Boys, we're just dancin' with death every time we go down that miserable mine shaft."

Joe and Ellen listened to some more complaining. It was clear that even though these Comstock miners were making good daily wages, it wasn't worth the great risks they were taking far underground.

Finally, Joe said, "I don't know any more about mining than I know about New York City, but it seems to me that you fellas are in a tough fix. Why don't you leave and go find work somewhere else?"

One of the miners snorted with derision. "Mister, you're right about not knowing mining. The simple answer to your question is that there are too many men and not enough work to go around on this strike. We're miners and this is where the mines are producing gold and silver, so this is where we have to be no matter how hard or dangerous the work."

"Well," Joe said, not wanting to inflame them any more than they already were, but determined to make a point, "once upon a time I was a free mountain man, a by gawd scalp-takin' fur trapper. But then, almost overnight, nobody wanted to buy beaver furs for hats anymore."

Joe threw up his hands as if he could snatch the answer to his problem from the air. "So, boys, I turned to what else I could do and that was leading wagon trains westward. And when that didn't quite work out, I became a freighter in Old Santa Fe. My point is that a man has to change his work sometimes or he's shit up a creek without a paddle."

"Well thank you, mister, for the damned lecture!" the one with the broken arm gritted between his bad teeth. "But we're here and we're miners and that's the long and the damned short of it! And by the way, this ain't any church and you ain't a preacher standing on a pulpit!"

Joe could feel his anger start to rise, but Ellen patted his arm and said, "I think I heard Dr. Taylor calling us to join him in that back room. Let's hope that I did and that Mr. McCarthy is alive."

"I'll second that sentiment," the miner with the broken arm snapped in exasperation. "So they can get that old bastard out of there and the doc can get back to fixin' me!"

Joe was about to slap the one-armed patient across the side of his head and then give his friends a go-around, when Dr. Taylor opened the door and motioned Joe and Ellen into the other room. Brendan McCarthy was asleep and his color had returned, although it was still poor.

"I've given him a strong dose of laudanum," the doctor explained, "although I can imagine that all he wants is more bad whiskey."

"What happened to him?"

"He told me that you hit him harder than

214

the kick of a Missouri mule," the doctor said, shaking his head and giving Joe a look of utter contempt. "You ought to be ashamed of yourself for behaving like that toward a man so much older and weaker than yourself."

"He's old," Joe agreed, "but he ain't a bit weak. And McCarthy wanted to choke me to death. He wasn't givin' me a friendly greeting, Doc."

"Well," Taylor said dismissively, "he's in extremely poor physical health. Undernourished. Probably got a bad liver from too many years of hard drinking, and he has a cough and lung infection with accompanying fever. Mr. McCarthy needs to be taken care of properly. If not, I doubt he'll last more than a few more weeks . . . possibly only days."

"We'll see to his care," Ellen said without a moment's hesitation.

Joe glared at her. "Ellen, what's the matter with you? That old goat ain't worth savin'."

"He's a child of *God*," Ellen countered. "Joe, it's the Christian thing to do. Do I need to remind you of what kind of condition you were in when you were found up —"

"All right. All right!" Joe finally conceded,

SOME PEOPLE!

215

knowing he couldn't honestly argue the point. "We'll see to him, but it's a waste of money. Even if McCarthy does pull through this time, he'll just go off on another long drunk and end up the same way."

"That doesn't matter to me," she told him. "I can only do what I can do with the Lord's good help. And yours, too, Joe. If you are truly willing to act in good faith and charity."

Joe took a moment to study McCarthy's rotgut-ravaged face. *Keep telling yourself how he's Fiona's father and you need him alive to find her and your daughter. He might be the only one who can help you find them now.*

"All right, Ellen," he heard himself say. "I'll do whatever needs to be done to help the old man."

"Thank you, Joe. I knew in my heart that you were a good man and would not abandon me or Mr. McCarthy and prove yourself to be anything less than a fine and godly man."

"Where can we take him, Doctor?"

"I know a widow who has a house on B Street. She is actually my sister-in-law and she'll help you to nurse this man through the worst of it. But it will cost you quite a lot of money."

"Everything costs a lot of money," Joe grumped. "Can we stay in the same house?"

"In separate rooms," Ellen quickly added.

"Of course," Joe agreed.

"I'm sure that would be acceptable, for the proper remuneration."

"The what?" Joe asked.

"Payment," Ellen said. "For the proper payment."

"I see. How much?"

"You will have to come to that arrangement with my sister-in-law. Her name is Mrs. Hamilton. Beth Hamilton. She's a widow and she has a fine house that is mostly empty."

"How far will I have to tote McCarthy this time?"

"I'll arrange for a wagon when he's regained consciousness. I'll also be coming by twice a day to check on his condition. Be advised that this man is hanging onto life by a thread."

"That's what I thought I was hanging by when he had me by the throat," Joe groused.

All this was really grinding hard on Joe. The last thing he wanted to do was to throw good money after bad on this old drunk. He hated Brendan McCarthy more than he'd ever hated any human being, but he needed him alive in order to find Fiona and his baby girl.

It was all just that damned simple.
Really.

20

"Quite a house, isn't it?" Ellen said as they stood before the two-story Victorian mansion owned by the widow Beth Hamilton. "Mr. Hamilton must have done very well before he died."

"I suppose," Joe answered, not impressed by houses. "Let's go in and see if the widow woman will let us stay here."

When they knocked on the door, Joe expected an elderly woman, but Mrs. Hamilton could not have been more than forty and she was quite attractive in a pleasingly plump sort of way. Joe stood back and let Ellen make the introductions and explain their need for rooms and care for the human wreckage that was Brendan McCarthy, and how Dr. Taylor, the widow's brother-in-law, had recommended them as possible tenants.

"You're asking quite a lot," Mrs. Hamilton said after hearing about their plight.

"Are you prepared to pay for it?"

Joe wasn't really, but Ellen said, "We are . . . if we can arrive at a reasonable fee. Dr. Taylor says that Mr. McCarthy is in very poor health. I'm not sure how much care he will need, but I will provide it so you will not be troubled with that responsibility."

Beth Hamilton studied Joe. "Sir, are you married?"

"No, ma'am," Joe said. "Ellen and I are just good friends."

Her eyebrows went up and she said, "I see."

Joe didn't know what that was supposed to mean, and he really didn't care. He could see through the doorway into Mrs. Hamilton's parlor, and it was way too damned prissy and pretty for his liking. He was thinking that he would go someplace else when the woman asked, "Joseph, are you skilled as a carpenter?"

"Nope."

She looked disappointed. "Then can you paint a wall or repair a roof?"

"I doubt it, ma'am. I'm just good with horses and other livestock."

"Well, you could at least help clean up around here."

But Joe shook his head. "Maybe I'll find another place to stay, Mrs. Hamilton. I ain't a servant and I ain't a yard man."

He started to leave, but the widow's voice carried sweetly to his ear. "I do have a horse in the backyard and his barn and corral are falling apart."

Joe turned around. "*You* have a horse?"

"It was my husband's, actually. He's a handsome brute. Big, rough, and strong like yourself. He hasn't been ridden in nearly a year and his name is Jasper. Do you think you could take care of fixing up his stable and exercising him under saddle?"

Joe removed his Stetson. "I'm no cowboy, Mrs. Hamilton, but I do know and like horses and mules. Sure, I could fix his corral and barn and ride the horse. Any chance that we could squeeze three more horses into your stable?"

"Why, Jasper would love some company! Of course, you'd have to expand the corral and barn, but I'd pay for the lumber since it would increase the value of this property."

This was sounding much better to Joe. "Ma'am," he said, breaking into a wide grin, "I think we can work this out fine."

"I will reduce your room and board for your help. Mrs. Johnson, are you willing to also help?"

"I am," Ellen said. "How much will you charge for all three of us and our three

221 SLOB!

horses?"

"If Joe will fix the corrals and expand the barn and you will help with cooking and cleaning, then I'll only ask twenty-five dollars a week, which includes food for your horses and yourselves."

"That is *very* generous," Ellen said, although Joe thought it outrageous.

Mrs. Hamilton clapped her hands together with happiness. "Actually, I do get lonely and this house is falling down around my poor shoulders, so I really would appreciate some help and company. My home has six bedrooms, three downstairs and three upstairs. You along with Mr. McCarthy will have the downstairs rooms and I very much look forward to meeting Mr. McCarthy."

You might change your mind when you lay your eyes on that mean and smelly old boar, Joe thought, wisely keeping his own counsel.

So it was arranged and they were shown impressive rooms on the mansion's ground floor. Joe had never stayed in anything nearly so grand and fancy. Why, the four-poster bed had a pink silk canopy, for gawd sake! And there were rugs on the floor and lace curtains. Golly, if his old Indian and trapper friends could only see him now! They would howl with laughter like a pack of wolves at the moon.

Around six o'clock, Dr. Taylor drove up to the mansion in his buggy with Brendan McCarthy slumped over on the seat. The besotted bastard was alive, but it was clear that he just hanging on by a thread. They got him into his room, and Joe let the women fuss over the old man while he and Dr. Taylor went outside with glasses of whiskey they'd poured in the kitchen.

"So," Taylor asked, "you are Joe Moss and that man is your father-in-law even though you smashed his face up with your fists."

They were sitting on a wide veranda overlooking the entire Comstock Lode and farther out, the Virginia City Cemetery, which was mighty large to Joe's way of thinking.

"Well, Doc, it's a complicated thing to explain and you'll be able to read a bunch more about it in tomorrow's edition of the *Territorial Enterprise.* But the long and short of it is that I have to find the woman I love, Fiona McCarthy . . . maybe now Fiona Moss . . . and my daughter, whose name I do not yet know."

"It does sound complicated," the doctor said. "And as I told you earlier, Mr. McCarthy could die at any moment from his poor health and heart trouble. So if you need to make amends or 'bury the hatchet,' so to speak, you ought to do it as soon as possible."

"I have nothing to make amends for to that man," Joe staunchly replied. "It was he that ruined my life and that of his daughter. That said, as soon as McCarthy tells me where to find Fiona, then he can go right ahead and die."

The doctor sipped his whiskey. "You're a hard man, Joe Moss. Not much compassion in you at all, is there?"

Joe frowned and sipped. "I've *had* to be a hard man to survive my entire lifetime. But now that I'm about to become the father of a four-year-old girl and the husband of the only woman I've ever really loved, I am probably going to soften up some around the edges."

"I hope so. What about Mrs. Johnson?"

"What about her?"

"She's a very attractive woman and I sense that she has real strength of character."

"Oh, she has plenty of that," Joe assured the doctor. "There are none better."

"Is she married?"

"Nope. She and her husband were Mormons and they had a fine farm down in Genoa. But Mr. Johnson died several years ago. All that is in the past and Ellen doesn't know where she wants to go or what she wants to do next."

"And you are in no way romantically involved with her?" Taylor asked, eyes fixed on the distant barren hills.

"Hell, no! I told you that I'm in love with that old man's daughter."

"Good," the doctor said with just the trace of a smile. "Glad to hear that, Joe."

Then the doctor finished his drink and left Joe on the porch so that he could go see McCarthy and, Joe suspected, Ellen as well.

Joe rocked and sipped Mrs. Hamilton's excellent rye whiskey. He was fascinated by the anthill of activity that stretched out before him. There were tailings more numerous than leaves on a tree, and he counted no less than eight huge mines with their smokestacks and huge tin buildings that Joe supposed housed massive steam engines, wheels, and hoisting works.

It was really all too much. Far too much busyness for Joe's liking, and he hoped that Fiona would not want to live here on the Comstock Lode once they were properly married. Better by far that they left this place and went off to the high mountains of Colorado or Wyoming, where he knew he could buy land by running water with aspen and pines for winter firewood. Or, if Fiona was averse to deep snow and cold, then Joe could take her south and find her warmer places down near Santa Fe and Taos where she could raise a garden and maybe some hogs to butcher.

"Mr. Moss?"

Joe was pulled out of his sweet reverie to see Mrs. Hamilton with a glass of whiskey in her own hand as well as the bottle. "May I replenish your drink?"

Joe had never had a drink "replenished," but it sounded like a good idea so he nodded.

"May I also join you?"

"Sure. It's your porch and view."

Beth Hamilton sat in the rocking chair just vacated by the doctor and looked out over the Comstock with a serene expression. "It's a view that I never tire of, Mr. Moss. Think of all the lives that are being lived out there and all the hopes and dreams that they represent. People come to our little mining town from all over the world and they have fascinating stories to tell."

"Yeah," Joe said, taking another slug of the excellent whiskey. "There's a whole lot of drunken miners, crooked gamblers, thieves, muggers, and hustlin' whores, that's for sure."

She glanced sideways at him with a frown

of annoyance. "There are also many *good* people down there, Mr. Moss."

"Joe," he corrected. "Just Joe, if you please, ma'am."

"All right, then you must call me Beth."

"Okay."

"I understand that you're seeking the woman you love and your little daughter."

"News spreads fast around here. But, yes, I am."

"I hope you find them as you have pictured them to be in your dreams."

Joe wasn't sure what the hell that meant, but the woman was nice, so he just nodded his head and kept rocking and admiring the view.

"Are you a Christian like Mrs. Johnson?"

"No, ma'am. But I'm not one to start tellin' the Bible lovers that they're wrong. Truth is, ma'am, I don't think anyone knows the truth about what happens after we ship out for the great unknown."

She was silent a few moments while considering his words. "I suppose that is a reasonable response, Joe. But not a very pleasant one."

"Life isn't supposed to be pleasant," he told her. "It's hard. Sometimes there are real fine moments when you're happy as a little chirpin' bird enjoyin' a fine spring morning, but mostly not."

"I have a very good life, even without my late husband. I am busy in women's societies and quite a few worthy charities. But I do miss a man's company."

"Well, you've two more men to deal with now." Joe stood up. "I'd like to go fetch our horses and put 'em up back there with Jasper. I already checked and you've got enough hay for 'em all for a week. After that, we'll buy you some more."

"And you've already fixed and expanded the corral fence?"

"I've done enough to make it do until I get more barbed wire, rails, and fence posts. For the time being it'll work out just fine."

"I'm so glad! Poor Jasper has been very lonely back there, and I'm sure that he's delighted to have the company of your nice horses."

Joe said nothing because Jasper had tried to cow-kick him in the head, and appeared to be a big, mean sonofabitch that wasn't worth feeding. But this woman obviously knew nothing about horses and she loved Jasper. Better just to let her cling to the illusion that he was a nice horse who welcomed the company of his own kind. And it was damn sure better not to tell her that his Palouse horse was gonna kick the hell outa Jasper and get him lined up properly in the pecking order about one minute after they met.

"Joe?"

It was Ellen at the doorway.

"Yeah?"

"Mr. McCarthy is awake and he wants to talk to you *in private.*"

"Humph!" Joe excused himself, drained his glass, and set it down on the railing before he went into McCarthy's room to confront the old man and learn the truth about Fiona's whereabouts.

"Close the door behind you," McCarthy ordered from his bed in a weak voice. "We have some serious talking to do."

"I reckon so," Joe replied, closing the door. "I come for Fiona and my child."

"You're too late."

Joe shut the door and went over to the old Irishman's bedside with his fists clenched at his sides. "It's never too late, Brendan. Now tell me where I can find 'em and don't give me any of your usual bullshit."

McCarthy's eyes shifted off toward the window, and damned if Joe didn't see that they were wet with fresh tears. He didn't think that the man had enough feelings for tears. McCarthy certainly hadn't shed any when his wife had died on the wagon train

229

that Joe had been leading westward four years earlier.

"Where are they?" Joe asked, his voice softening.

"I don't know where Fiona is now," McCarthy replied. "Honest to God I don't."

Joe swallowed his disappointment like it was a rough rock. "What about my child?"

"You have a daughter. Her name is Jessica."

"Jessica," he whispered. "That's a real pretty name."

"Not half as pretty as she is," McCarthy told him. "She and Fiona are the lights of my sorry life."

"Where is the girl?"

McCarthy hesitated for so long that Joe almost grabbed him by the neck to shake the truth out of the old man. But then he said, "Joe, you're not going to like this one little bit, but your daughter Jessica is in the care of the Sisters of Charity down at the Catholic church."

Joe was stunned. "But . . . but *why?*"

"Because Fiona *gave* Jessica to them. They are now her legal guardians."

"To hell if they are!" Joe roared.

"I told you that you wouldn't like it, but that's the truth. Little Jessica lives at the convent down at St. Mary of the Mountain, and she's being raised in the Catholic faith and expected to take her vows someday and join their order."

Joe staggered over to an expensive sitting chair and fell into it half-dazed. "You mean become a *nun!*"

"Yep. That's how it's going to be."

"Over my dead body!" Joe shouted, coming to his feet again.

McCarthy looked up at the stricken expression on Joe's face, and then he cackled with crazy, broken laughter and sobs of despair.

"They won't even let me visit her," McCarthy finally said. "They run me off and told me never to come back."

"They won't run me off, by gawd!"

"By gawd they will," McCarthy countered. "Those nuns mother that girl like hens do their chicks. As far as they are concerned, everyone and everything in little Jessica's past was sent by Satan. They're going to save her soul and shield her from all evil."

McCarthy took a deep, ragged breath and scrubbed at his wet eyes. "I'm evil and you're evil. And to them, even Fiona is evil."

"I'll go get her!" Joe vowed. "I'll go get her right now."

"You can try," McCarthy told him. "But

you won't have any more luck at it than I did."

"What? You think I can't handle nuns?"

The old man shook his head. "Fiona gave them legal custody of Jessica. She was desperate and on the run. It was what she thought best to do."

"What do you mean, 'on the run'?" Joe demanded.

"I mean she was running for her life," McCarthy said. "Because she killed Mr. Chester J. Peabody."

"No! Fiona wouldn't kill anybody."

"I'm sure that she had no choice." McCarthy sobbed and stiffened with pain. He shuddered and wheezed. "You see, Joe, Fiona had. . . ."

Suddenly, the Irishman's eyes went round with fear and overwhelming pain. He gasped and grabbed at his chest, mouth working silently in a desperate plea for something that Joe could only imagine.

"Doc!" Joe shouted. "Doc!"

Dr. Taylor was at the bedside in a moment. But it was too late. Brendan McCarthy's heart had failed completely and he was already dead.

21

"Joe? Joe!" Ellen shouted, but Joe was already trotting down the mountainside headed for the tall, white-steepled St. Mary's. He didn't exactly know what he was going to say or do, but he had to see his daughter and no one was going to hold him back from that after all these years.

Joe had long legs and halfway down the mountainside, he realized that he had left all his weapons in his room at the Hamilton mansion. Probably just as well. The last thing he needed to do was to kill a nun or a priest. That, by gawd, would get him hanged and sent to hell for certain.

The church was very impressive, and sat just below the town on a large lot next to a sign that proclaimed in bold letters that this would be the future home of the Virginia and Truckee Railroad. Joe could read that sign, but it held no interest for him. He stopped a few hundred feet from the big, brick church and rectory, then took a few deep breaths to calm down.

McCarthy said that Fiona had given the nuns the legal right to raise our child. Now why on earth would she have done a thing like that? Fiona wasn't a Catholic! But if what that old man said before he died was true, I have to be on my best behavior. If I go in there shouting and with blood in my eye, then it'll only make getting Jessica back all the tougher.

Joe smoothed out his clothes and wished that he could hide McCarthy's bloodstains from when he'd carried the old drunk over to Dr. Taylor's office. But the bloodstains were dried and set into his shirt, and there was nothing to do for it unless he wanted to hike back up the mountainside and find a mercantile, then buy himself a new shirt.

Maybe I should do that, he thought, suddenly very unsure of himself because what happened next with the nuns might be the most important meeting of his entire life.

"Joe!"

He turned to see Ellen hurrying after him, and he waited for her because he was suddenly unsure of what to say to the nuns or how to ask for Jessica.

"Joe," she said, badly out of breath, "what are you doing?"

"My daughter is in there with 'em, Ellen,

234

and they're fixin' to make her one of their kind. Take the vows and everything."

"But your daughter is only four years old."

"They start 'em young. When I was in Santa Fe, I saw those priests and nuns and they had those little Mexican kids bowin' and makin' the sign of the cross almost before they were off the teat."

Ellen took his hand. "Listen to me carefully. I'm your friend and you trust my judgment, don't you?"

"Sure, but. . . ."

"Then I'm telling you that this isn't the way to handle the situation."

"But. . . ."

"We'll go back up to the mansion and talk about this. Come up with a plan of action. That way, when we meet these good Catholic nuns, we've got everything in mind that we need to say and know. We've thought it out, Joe."

"Don't you understand that I've waited four years for this moment?" Joe said with exasperation.

"Then you can wait a few hours more so that we don't make this harder than it should be. Most likely, the nuns will understand that you are Jessica's father and have a right to reclaim her."

"But what if they don't?"

"Well, Joe, you can't use your fists, knife, gun, or tomahawk on them. You understand that, don't you?"

"I reckon," he said with a heavy heart.

"If they won't let Jessica go, then we can hire a lawyer to help us."

"I don't put much faith in 'em, Ellen."

"Perhaps not, but that's our best option. We can ask Mrs. Hamilton and that newspaperman, Dan DeQuille, who is the best lawyer in Virginia City. But maybe it won't come to that. It probably won't. Let's just calm down and go back to the mansion and think this out so that we make a good first impression on the priest and his nuns."

Joe knew that Ellen was right. "I need to buy a new shirt and coat. Maybe take another bath and get a shave, too."

"Now you're talking," Ellen said, linking her arm with his and slowly turning Joe around. "What did Mr. McCarthy say about Fiona before he died of heart failure?"

Joe stopped and took a deep breath. "He said that Fiona *killed a man*."

Ellen's hand tightened her grip. "That's what he said?"

"Yes. A man named Chester J. Peabody. He sounded like an important fella 'cause he put *Mister* in front of the name."

"That doesn't make sense to me," Ellen

said. "If Fiona did that, then surely Mr. De-Quille, Dr. Taylor, or Mrs. Hamilton would have heard about it."

"I don't know what to tell you," Joe said, shaking his head in confusion. "But I have to believe that old man McCarthy was telling me the truth. Besides, I know Fiona, and she wouldn't have abandoned our daughter unless something terrible had gone wrong."

Ellen thought about it a moment, then said, "There are only two explanations. One is that Mr. DeQuille, Beth Hamilton, and the doctor didn't make the connection because Fiona was using your last name, Moss, instead of McCarthy. And the other is that no one knows for sure who killed Mr. Peabody."

"Somebody knows," Joe said. "Otherwise, Fiona wouldn't have had to run for her life."

"That's right. That's exactly right. So we need to find out who knows about this death and what this all means for Fiona and your daughter."

Joe removed his hat and sleeved his sweating brow. For some reason he felt drawn to the cemetery. "Maybe Peabody is lyin' in his grave right over there. Maybe it would tell us something."

"Headstones don't usually state the cause

of death, but we can hike over there and take a look," Ellen suggested. "We have time to do that before sundown."

Joe stared hard at the church, almost as if his eyes could penetrate those red brick walls and see his little girl at last. But they couldn't, of course, so he shrugged and said, "Let's go ahead and try that. The walk to the cemetery will help clear my troubled mind."

Ellen took his hand and they headed off, but neither one of them was optimistic that the cemetery would hold the answer to this tragic mystery that had just turned all of their worlds upside down.

22

It was an even bigger cemetery than Joe had thought after viewing it from a long distance. There were, of course, separate sections for the Catholics and the Protestants, and a third section off in the back that was on the steepest, rockiest ground where Indians, Mexicans, and the Chinese were buried.

"We'll start in the Protestant section," Ellen said as they stepped through the wrought-iron gate and entered the cemetery. "If we don't find a Peabody there, we'll go to the Catholic section."

Joe thought that sounded like a reasonable plan. He didn't feel comfortable hanging around in a cemetery no matter what the former faith of the people it held. But as they moved around in the Protestant section, he began to appreciate how dangerous and unhealthy it was to be a deep-rock miner on the Comstock Lode.

"Almost all of these graves are only two and three years old," Ellen observed. "And most of them are as humble as apple pie. Look, Joe, many of the tombstones tell the story of where these poor people came from, and a few even tell *why* they died."

"William McCord," Joe read from a headstone. *"Born in County Cork, Ireland, in 1838. Died of a mine cave-in. Bill was a friend to all."* Joe shook his head. "Poor Bill McCord was just twenty-four years old when he died."

"Most of these men were only in their twenties," Ellen said, her expression sad. "Mine cave-ins, mine floods, poisonous gas, and pneumonia."

"And some died from drinkin' like McCarthy," Joe said. "Quite a few, in fact."

"And look," Ellen said, "how many are from England and Wales."

"Here's a young woman named Nora," Joe said. "And she's buried beside her baby, Andrew Parks. Looks like she was just a girl herself and her poor child wasn't but a day old."

"Nora Parks died in childbirth, Joe. It happens all the time because the unborn baby is turned the wrong way or there's bleeding that can't be stopped. Maybe other things that I don't care to explain."

"At least Fiona didn't die havin' Jessica," Joe said, trying to boost his low spirits. "And I sure wish that I'd have been there at her side."

"Women don't want men at their side in childbirth unless they have no choice."

"They don't?"

"No," Ellen said. "When bringing a child into the world, a woman wants another woman who knows what to do and how it feels."

"How would you know?"

Joe instantly regretted the question for he could see the hurt in Ellen Johnson's eyes. "Sorry," he said.

"That's all right. I never was blessed with a child, but I did help bring many a baby into this world kicking and screaming. And a few that were stillborn, too."

Joe nodded with understanding, and then he heard a wagon coming and turned to see that it was a black hearse pulled by a black horse. The driver was dressed all in black with a top hat, and the hearse was followed by several people on foot. One of them appeared to be a grieving widow. Joe watched the hearse and mourners shuffle past and then enter the Catholic section. A grave was waiting with a fresh mound of dirt ready to toss over the dead husband.

"Here is our Mr. Peabody!" Ellen called, bringing Joe's attention back to the matter at hand. "That's quite an elaborate monument. Much more impressive than any others nearby."

"Impressive" was an understatement. Chester Peabody's monument stood at least six feet tall with a cross at the top and a lot of fancy engravings of flowers and angels on the wing. Joe bet the thing probably cost more than a horse and wagon and that it easily weighed a couple of tons.

"And look what it says, Joe. Read it out loud."

"Chester J. Peabody, born Dec. 12, 1821 in Philadelphia, Pa. Died March 21, 1862. May our brother Chester's soul sing in Heaven and may his murderer's soul burn forever in Hell."

"What's 'Pa' mean?" Joe asked.

"Pennsylvania," Ellen answered. "So Chester was murdered and it's obvious that his family is very hurt and bitter."

"Ain't too surprisin'," Joe replied. "But the question I want answered is, who are these family people and do they think that my Fiona murdered their Chester?"

"I would guess that the family would not be difficult to locate. The grave is only a few months old and the headstone is expensive enough to tell us that this family has a good deal of money."

Joe studied the tall, impressive headstone and the mound of dirt decorated with small quartz rocks and protected by a very ornate iron fence of solid construction and intricate design. Joe put his hand on the fence, which had little spikes every foot, and said, "This fence will last a couple hundred years, at least. And the headstone will last even longer."

"Yes. And those flowers by the headstone aren't more than a few days old, Joe. So that means that someone is visiting this grave often."

Joe sighed. "I sure don't see how Peabody's murder could be connected to Fiona."

"But it must be," Ellen said. "And we just need to ask around to find out where we can find the Peabody family."

"I expect so," Joe replied, seeing an old man with some wilted flowers trudging up the path toward them. He limped through the gate and came to one of the graves nearby, where he removed his battered hat, lowered himself to his knees, bowed his head, and began to pray. Joe could see tears on his wrinkled cheeks, and when he was through praying, the old man placed the wilted flowers on the grave, which bore only a simple wooden cross.

When the old man was finished, he looked over at Joe and Ellen and said, "You come to pay your respects to Mr. Peabody, did you?"

"I'm afraid we never had the pleasure of knowing the man," Ellen replied. "But he must have been quite prominent and successful. His monument is the largest in this cemetery."

"He was a very rich and important man. A family man and very much respected here on the Comstock Lode. I guess he belonged to about every organization in Virginia City and he was always generous with his charity. When he was murdered, the whole town turned out for the funeral. Even the volunteer fire department marched by his hearse and the Masonic Lodge was out in full force. There was a marching band and a lot of words of farewell. Must have been fifty bouquets of flowers sent all the way over from Sacramento. So many they covered Mr. Peabody's coffin and then his grave."

The old man bit his lower lip and swallowed hard. "I am ashamed to say that the day after Mr. Peabody's funeral, I stole a big bouquet of flowers and placed them on my sweet Emma's grave. Guess that makes me a thief."

Ellen hurried over to the grieving old man. "No, it doesn't. And I'm sure that Mr. Peabody, God rest his soul, was pleased to give your Emma flowers for her grave."

Ellen's words were so kind that the old codger began to bawl. Joe didn't know what to do, so he turned and looked away while Ellen comforted the man and got him calmed down.

"I'm sorry," the man said. "I just haven't been able to get over losing her. We were married for forty-three years. I never should have brought her up here to Virginia City. It's freezing in the winter and blazing hot in the summers. Bad water. Bad ground and bad people, for the most part."

"How did Mr. Peabody come to meet his death?" Joe asked, unable to contain his curiosity.

"He was murdered one night. His body was found outside a little shack up on D Street where a woman by the name of Moss lived with her young daughter."

Joe grew very still. Ellen took his hand and squeezed it hard saying, "Sir, could you tell me any more about the murder?"

"Why do you want to know?"

Ellen said, "Because this is Joe Moss and he was . . . is . . . looking for his . . . wife."

The old man stared at Joe. "Peabody's

murderer was your wife?"

"In a manner of speaking," Joe said, not wishing to tell the man that he had deflowered Fiona while leading her family westward in a wagon train.

The old man shook his head and his voice turned hard with anger. "Your wife, sir, was a whore and a murderess. I am sorry, but as God is my witness, she murdered poor Mr. Peabody and gave up her child to flee for her life."

Joe started to protest that Fiona would never have done such a thing, but Ellen cut him off saying, "Joe Moss is a good man who had nothing to do with the death of Mr. Peabody. He has come to claim his child, who we understand is a girl now in the custody of the Catholic nuns."

"That's right. And they'll bring her up to eat mackerel on Fridays and pray for the Pope, but she'll never be a whore and she'll never murder anybody like her mother did to poor Mr. Peabody."

"How do people know for certain that it was Mrs. Moss who murdered Mr. Peabody?" Joe finally was able to ask.

"Who else could have done it? There was blood all over the inside of that woman's shack, and even a bloody butcher knife resting on the table. She stabbed him to death and he must have tried to get away, but she stabbed him in the back until he collapsed outside her door."

The old man was getting upset, and Joe didn't want to hear another lying word out of his mouth, so he just turned and headed down the path toward Virginia City.

Sometimes, a man had to step away from something before he took it in his hands and killed it for being a lie.

23

Joe didn't sleep at all well that night. Once, he had gotten up and crept silently out on the porch to sit in the rocking chair and stare down at the lights of Virginia City. Most of the lights had been extinguished, but there were enough to remind him of a swarm of prairie fireflies. The hills surrounding the town were dotted with the dying campfires of the men who lived out in the brush unable to pay for a bed and a roof over their heads. And down on C Street, the impressive Bucket of Blood, Silver Dollar, and Delta saloons were always busy. Even from a quarter mile off, Joe could hear the faint tinkling of out-of-tune pianos and coarse, drunken laughter. Once, he heard a ragged scream followed by two rapid gunshots. Joe was pretty sure someone new was going to soon take up permanent residence in the Virginia City Cemetery.

To Joe's way of thinking, things just hadn't

gone all that well since he'd arrived on the Comstock. Oh, sure, he and Ellen had fallen into some luck by getting this fine place to live and to board their three horses. That had been a true stroke of good fortune, but it paled beside the fact that his Fiona was missing and now considered a murderess. Almost as distressing to Joe was that he had a little girl that he might not be able to claim as his own flesh and blood.

The more that he thought about it, he realized that he had no proof whatsoever that little Jessica Moss was his child. He had no marriage certificate binding himself to her mother. No one down at that Catholic church had ever even seen or heard of Joe Moss. True, Fiona had taken his last name, yet Joe doubted that would stand up in any court of law as proof that he was Jessica's father.

So he rocked in the moonlight and he smoked and thought about sneaking into Beth Hamilton's kitchen and getting that half-filled bottle of whiskey. If he drank it all, he might eke out a few hours of sleep, but he'd have bloodshot eyes in the morning and his head would be full of wet wool.

About five o'clock in the morning, Joe went back to bed and managed to sleep until seven. Then, clear-headed but tired and fretful over what was to come later, he got dressed and trudged downtown, where he had a solitary breakfast, then got a shave. When the stores opened at nine o'clock, he bought a new shirt and pair of pants. Then he trudged back up to the mansion and took a bath.

"I'm ready," he announced about eleven o'clock that morning. "Might as well go down and face those pious mackerel-snappers."

"We're going with you," Ellen announced. "Beth says that although she is not Catholic, she does know Father O'Connor and has a nodding acquaintance with several of St. Mary's nuns."

"All right," Joe agreed, glad to have their company. "Then let's get to it. I've waited a long, long time to see my child."

Beth Hamilton grabbed her bonnet and shawl although the morning was not that cool. "Joe," she said, choosing her words with care, "you *are* the girl's father, but Ellen and I would like to do most of the talking and explaining."

Joe was instantly annoyed. "Why?" he demanded. "Don't you *educated* ladies think I'm good enough to stand on my own damned feet and claim my own blood?"

"No, no!" Ellen said, trying to placate

him. "That's not it at all."

Joe stubbornly shook his head like a big dog with a bone. He banged on his chest with a closed fist. "Look! I've had a bath so I smell good. I've had a shave that cost me two bits and I'm wearin' these stiff new duds that feel like newspaper. Why, I even polished my new boots!"

"You look very nice," Beth told him. "Very handsome indeed. But. . . ."

"But what!" he snapped, eyes blazing.

"Joe," Ellen said gently, "Beth and I have been talking about this all morning and trying to think of the best arguments to make for you getting legal custody of Jessica. And one of the things that we're sure of is that the clergy down at St. Mary's will be very concerned about the religious upbringing of your daughter. In fact, that will probably be their greatest objection to giving her up to you."

Joe was angry, but he had to admit the truth of it. "Well," he said with a troubled expression, "I won't tell the Catholics that there isn't a God, because there just might be. And I won't tell them Holy Rollers there ain't no Devil, because I've seen Satan's work many a time in my own sorry life. But I ain't gonna buy that child no rosary beads or Bible and —"

"Joe, listen to me!" Ellen interrupted. "Beth and I agree that, if we're to have any chance of getting that child back to you, that you're going to have to agree to become a Catholic and bring Jessica up in the Catholic faith."

"The hell you say!" Joe bellowed in shock and outrage and stomped the floor with his boot so hard the dishes danced. "Ain't no way that is ever gonna happen!"

Beth and Ellen exchanged glances before Ellen said, "Then we will probably have to get a lawyer, and that will be expensive and most likely futile."

Joe glared at them both. "Are you sayin' that unless I become a Catholic I might not ever get Jessica back?"

"That's exactly what we are saying," Beth told him as she folded her arms across her ample bosom. "And we think it's important that you understand that before you face Father O'Connor and his order of nuns."

Joe swore under his breath and turned away, feeling like he wanted to punch holes in the walls or maybe kick a few stray dogs and cats. Instead, he turned around and said, "Ladies, I'm a sinner through and through, and I just don't think I can ever join any church, and most especially the Catholic Church."

Ellen's face was pinched and set. "You just might have to, Joe. You might have to if you want your little girl."

Joe tore off his hat and slapped the wall a few times in frustration. "Dammit, the talkin' is done here. Let's go see Jessica."

The heavy double wooden doors of the church were wide open to let in the fresh morning air, and Joe and the two women stood in the front of the church looking down the aisle toward the altar as a small nun in her fifties came to greet them with a gentle smile.

"Why, Mrs. Hamilton," she said. "So good to see you. It's been a long time."

"Yes it has. Sister Barbara, these are my friends."

Joe looked up toward the impressive altar, admiring it and smelling the many candles that were burning in red jars. There were a few people already kneeling in the pews prayin' for all that they were worth, and Joe figured that their sins combined weren't anything compared to his own. He saw a big organ up front and lots of statues of saints. This was a holy place, and the anger that had been building inside of him all the way down the hill evaporated.

"Mr. Joseph Moss has come to see his

daughter, Jessica," Beth was explaining while the nun now stared at Joe as if he were a messenger of Satan. "And I know this is all very sudden and difficult, Sister, but we do need to see the girl and discuss how soon Mr. Moss can take her into his loving custody and care."

The nun made the sign of the cross. She looked about to faint. Joe started to reach out and support her, but she backed away as if he might bite.

Finally, Sister Barbara cleared her voice and said, "I think that Mr. Moss needs to see Father O'Connor."

"That would be a good idea," Beth said, trying to smile.

"Please follow me," the nun said, making the sign of the cross again and then heading up the aisle.

Joe had to be pushed into the church by the women, and he was almost shaking until the nun veered into a big room where an old priest was having tea with several nuns.

"Father, this is Mr. Joseph Moss," the nun announced. "He has come to take our Jessica because he . . . he is claiming *father-hood*."

The nuns let out a collective gasp. Father O'Connor spilled tea on himself, and there was a heavy silence that seemed to last forever. Finally, the old Irish priest managed to smile and said, "Dear friends, please sit down and share a cup of tea and a pastry with us this morning."

Ellen and Beth joined them at the table, but Joe couldn't move his feet, so he said, "I have been waiting four years to find out whether I fathered a boy or girl with sweet Fiona McCarthy. I'd sure like to see my daughter right now . . . if it is okay with you."

"I'm afraid that it is not 'okay,' " the priest said softly as he clasped his hands together so tight that the knuckles went bloodless. "Mr. Moss, I feel that we need to have a quiet conversation . . . just the two of us. Father to father."

"Okay," Joe said, looking around for a place to go off with the priest.

"Sister Barbara, would you please pour these dear ladies tea and give them refreshments while Mr. Moss and I go have a pleasant little conversation?" O'Connor suggested.

All the nuns nodded in unison.

Joe followed the priest through a narrow hallway into a small room with a table, chair, and bookcase filled with titles he could not begin to read and whose religious concepts he could never hope to comprehend.

"Please have a chair, Mr. Moss. Are you by chance one of our faith?"

"No, sir."

"A Protestant, then?"

"Not that, either."

"Please sit down, Mr. Moss."

Joe sat stiffly. Heart hammering. He had a feeling he had lost this argument before he had even had a chance to speak his true heart and mind.

Father O'Connor took a moment to compose himself and perhaps to say a quick prayer for the right words. Then he began with a question. "Mr. Moss, are you aware of the circumstances that have blessed us with the presence and responsibility of Jessica? How her mother came to us in the dead of the night with bloody hands and gave us this child begging that we love and protect her?"

Joe stammered, "I don't know. . . ."

"Mr. Moss, we agreed to love and protect little Jessica because this is a haven, a sanctuary . . . a *holy place* filled with charity and spiritual grace. But we did ask only one thing in return for our promise to take in that child, and that was that we be given full legal custody until Jessica was twenty-one years of age. I have the document that Fiona Moss or McCarthy signed, and the page has a drop of her own blood to seal this covenant."

Joe started to protest, but the priest held up his hand silencing Joe's tongue. "Mr. Moss," he continued, "I have no doubt that you have the very best of intentions for that beautiful child of God. That you think you love her even though you have never been her father and have never even seen Jessica. However, for the sake of the child both physically and spiritually, I must insist that you not only do not try to take her, but that you have no contact whatsoever with Jessica. It would only cause her pain and confusion . . . both of which she has had to suffer already because of the tragic circumstances surrounding her mother."

"But. . . ."

"I must *insist,* Mr. Moss! There can be no possibility of reconciliation."

Joe cleared his voice. "I will do whatever it takes, Father. I just have to have that girl who is of *my* blood, not the Church's."

"We are *all* God's beloved children and members of the one Church," O'Connor said, "only some have not yet been shown the true path to eternal salvation."

"I just want to have Jessica!"

"I'm very, very sorry."

Joe jumped up. "Listen, priest, I demand that you give up that girl!"

"Never." O'Connor's voice had changed to steel. "Not even if you killed me this very moment would I give her up to a heathen who is not even a Christian."

Joe began to shake. "Where is she right now!"

The priest shook his head, lips pressed tightly together.

Joe whirled and ran from the room. He heard voices calling him, but he kept running down hallways searching, searching room after small, spartan room, until at last he burst into a space where a very old nun was reading a book to a very small and beautiful girl with hair as black as a raven's wing and eyes as large and luminous as a harvest moon.

"Jessica. Jessica!"

She smiled, and Joe found himself on his knees with tears streaming down his cheeks.

The old nun closed her book and then took the child in her arms, her billowy black habit almost engulfing Jessica.

"Dear sir, you are *upsetting* this sweet, innocent child," she said with firmness but without anger. "Please go away."

Joe found himself nodding and crying and

258

backing up on his knees through the doorway with his eyes fixed on his daughter. The girl's eyes were round . . . not with fear . . . but with curiosity, and then she glanced up at the nun for some explanation and perhaps reassurance.

"God bless you, now go *away*," the nun said, rising to close the door and shut out the only light now left in Joe Moss's streaming eyes.

24

Joe Moss got blind drunk that afternoon, and he stayed that way for twenty-four hours, until Beth and Ellen threatened to shoot him and then throw him down an abandoned mine shaft.

"Joe," Ellen scolded, "getting drunk just isn't going to help get Jessica back or figure out how you can find Fiona. And just because that high-priced lawyer that Mr. DeQuille recommended told you that you had no hope of winning in court, that shouldn't mean that you just give up."

"What else is there to do?" Joe said with a groan as he forced down a strong cup of coffee that Beth Hamilton had given him. "My wife is wanted for murder and my daughter might as well be locked up in a prison for all the good it does me."

"That's not true about Jessica. She is in a safe and loving place where you don't have to worry about her. The thing to do now is to sober up and go to work on getting them both back."

"How?" he asked, hands a little shaky on the coffee cup.

"Beth and I have been talking about that while you were getting sloshed, and we think the best thing for you to do is to make a lot of money on the Comstock Lode so that when Fiona returns for Jessica . . . and you know that she will . . . you'll have the financial means to hire not just one, but a team of the best lawyers that money can buy. If you can do that, I'm sure that you can win both Fiona and Jessica back."

Joe almost wanted to laugh out loud at the ridiculous suggestion. "Sure," he said, "what I'll do is stake a claim about six miles from here along with the other poor prospectors, then strike it rich right away. That'll work, won't it?"

Ellen wasn't amused. "You are a man of many abilities and we will be your advisors. Why not give it a try? The alternative is just to stay drunk and give up on your wife and daughter. Are you a *quitter,* Joe Moss?"

His chin snapped up. "Ladies, I've never been a quitter. I've often been a failure, but it wasn't because I didn't try."

"Then let's get you started," Beth said.

"On what?"

The two women exchanged glances and Ellen said, "First, you need to know a little about mining. That means you have to go down in a mine and —"

"No!" Joe shouted. "I won't go down on one of those cages."

"Well, then," Beth said, "I guess that our plan for you goes out the window. You might as well move out of here and stay drunk."

"Why do I have to move out?"

"Because I won't tolerate a drunkard," Beth Hamilton said. "And neither of us wants to watch you go the way of poor Brendan McCarthy."

Joe was sitting back on the veranda in the rocking chair, and although his stomach was sour and his brain felt busted, as he gazed down on Virginia City and all the little camps and hardships, he realized he didn't want to go down there and try to make a living. So he was either going to accept the plan these women had for him and trust that they were right . . . or he was going to get on his horse and leave the Comstock Lode far behind. Only thing was, if he left, he would never see his wife and daughter again.

Ever.

"All right," he said, giving in. "I'll go down and do some deep, hard-rock mining. But I don't know how I'm going to get hired. There are a lot of experienced miners begging for jobs."

"I know important people who own and operate some of the best mines," Beth told him. "We can get you a job."

"How long do I have to do it?"

"A month ought to teach you all you need to know about finding and extracting gold and silver."

Joe bent his head and shook it sadly. "When do I have to start?"

"I'll make the arrangements tomorrow for you to go on the noon-until-midnight shift at the Belcher Mine."

Joe had the strongest urge to get drunk all over again, but he didn't. He'd need every bit of his mental and physical ability in order to survive deep under this mountain where men were dying every day, some never to be found.

It was almost noon and Joe was standing on the loading platform waiting his turn to go down to the eight-hundred-foot level. Joe had been given a miner's hat with a candle, and a pick had been shoved into his fists. There were five other men in the same group that was to be lowered in the cage, and the surrounding din from the heavy steam engines and massive machinery in the hoisting works was louder than a locomotive going through a train tunnel.

Joe wanted to ask these men what it was going to feel like when they were lowered down on the cable, but it was too noisy to be heard, so he just stepped onto the little cage, gripped its center bar, and closed his eyes.

Suddenly, the world seemed to drop away as if he'd stepped off a cliff. Joe felt weightless, and his stomach pushed up hard against his hammering heart, and the cage gathered speed on its wild plummet into darkness. As the cage shot downward, it passed cavernous work stations where, for just an instant, he saw bare-chested miners. Then there was more darkness, followed by a quick glimpse of another level and another.

Finally, the cage came to a hard, springy stop, and Joe thought he was going to vomit on the other men packed up against him. But he was shoved off the slightly bouncing cage, and tumbled face-first into a cavern, which was about the size of a boxcar. Five weary and blackened miners took Joe's place in the bouncing cage and disappeared toward the sun.

"Get up," the mine shift foreman ordered.

"We got a lot of work to be done today on the south face. Moss, light your candle and get steady on your feet."

Joe climbed unsteadily to his feet. The air was very hot and it tasted foul. He immediately began to sweat and feel sick. He looked up and then around the work station next to the main shaft, wondering if it was going to collapse in on him at any moment.

"It's called square setting," the foreman explained. "In most mines they support the ceilings with what is called 'post-and-cap' timbering, which looks like a whole line of doorframes. Other mines I've worked in Colorado use what's called a 'room-and-pillar' method in which thick columns of ore are left standing to support the heavy weight of the ceilings. But what you're looking at down this deep is called 'square-set timbering,' which was invented by this bright young German mining engineer named Philipp Deidesheimer. Because this Comstock Lode rock down here is porous and expands when exposed to the air, we were having so many cave-ins that we couldn't work at this depth. But Deidesheimer came up with this square-set timbering using short, massive timbers and tyin' 'em together in blocks or cubes. Each cube can be interlocked with the next one forming what you see all around you now."

The foreman smiled. "It kinda looks a honeycomb, doesn't it?"

Joe nodded, too stupefied by his dizzying descent and first impression of this unearthly work station even to speak.

"All right, Moss," the foreman said, taking no more time to admire the engineering, "you've had your lesson for today. Now it's time for us to get to work."

Joe struggled to his feet and lit the candle stuck to his metal helmet. The miners all carried picks and shovels as they trudged along a narrow tunnel supported by miniature square sets. Joe followed his crew, feeling the sweat running off his chest, back, and shoulders to soak into his pants.

They followed a pair of narrow-gauge iron rails, and most of the time the tunnel's ceiling was so low that they had to stoop and duck in order to move forward. Joe's back was bent at the waist and it soon began to ache. The rock walls seemed to close in tighter and tighter, so that Joe found himself fighting off claustrophobia.

At last, they came to a small cavern where the foreman pointed to the wall and told Joe and three of his crew to start busting loose ore. The rest of the crew was led farther down the tunnel to work another face.

"Just be careful not to send that pick through the wall into a pocket of scalding water," the miner next to Joe warned. "If you do that, we're all gonna get boiled."

"How do I know if there's water on the other side of this rock wall?" Joe asked, pick raised.

"If you live long enough down here, then you'll learn to tell by the sound of your pick striking the rock. If it sounds hollow or starts to get too soft, back away fast and give a holler to the rest of us. The ore that you bust off this wall gets tossed in that little mine car on the tracks. When they're loaded, we take turns pushing it back to the shaft, where it's sent up in the cage we came down on. Got it?"

Joe nodded and began to work. He was strong and his hands were calloused, yet they were soon stinging with fresh blisters. He started out too fast, and was soon gasping like a beached fish and unable to get his breath in the thin, fetid air whose temperature was about 110 degrees.

"Pace yourself, Moss," the foreman told him as he came by. "Steady and strong. Twenty blows a minute is a good rate to work up to. Take it easy the first few days.

It'll come to you after about a week."

I won't last a damned week, Joe thought, sweat burning his eyes and his spine feeling as if it was going to snap like a stick.

At the end of the twelve-hour shift in hell, Joe could hardly straighten his back when they climbed onto the cage for the fast ascent up to the hoisting works. He clung to the cage and left his stomach somewhere deep in the mine. When the cage burst out into the big, tin-roofed building, all the same machinery was clanging and banging. But the air was good again, and he could see patches of dark sky through the tall rusting tin roof.

"You did good, Moss," his shift boss said, patting Joe on the shoulder. "It'll get easier day by day. See you in twelve hours."

Joe didn't think he would come back, but he did. He came back for eleven straight days with blistered hands and dread in his heart. Several times while down below, he had heard of other men working on other levels, some as deep as a thousand feet, who had been crushed by cave-ins that even square-set timbering could not completely eliminate.

And then, on the twelfth day, a more

seasoned miner on Joe's crew named John Barton from England punched a hole through a crumbly wall. Instantly, a stream of boiling water burst out of an adjoining cavern to scald him right where he stood with his pick stuck tight.

Joe wasn't standing five feet from Barton, and had grown to like the young man and respect his endurance and hard work. But now Barton was screaming and rolling on the ground, and men were grabbing him to run at a crouch down the long tunnel to the main work station. They could hear the roar of the hot water as it shot through and widened the hole, then began to pour down the tunnel.

Joe was right there helping to drag and carry the howling Englishman. "What do we do now!" he yelled when they stood beside the cable that told them the cage was dangling hundreds of feet below.

"We signal for it to take us up and out of here!" the foreman cried. "And we wait to see how much hot water is coming down that tunnel after us. If it's huge, we'll all either boil or be swept down the shaft. If it's a small reservoir, maybe we'll live."

Joe and the others listened to the hot water come coursing down the tunnel in a wave about three feet high. In the feeble light of their cap-candles they saw that it was black and oily-looking as men tried to jump onto the mine cart so that their feet, ankles, and lower legs would not be burned.

Joe pushed the already scalded Englishman into the cart, and took a running jump, grabbing the thick, twisted mine cable just as the steaming water hit the vertical shaft and showered downward for hundreds of feet. He clung to the cable, lost in a cloud of hissing steam, hearing men screaming far, far down below.

How long Joe clung to the cable before the water receded, he did not know. Maybe it was only for a few minutes. But when it was over, he looked back into the work station and saw the rest of his shift piled into the ore cart like terrified rats clinging to a sinking ship.

"All right," the mine crew foreman said at last when the water had all but disappeared down the shaft. "Let's see if we can get back to work. It looks like that pocket of water wasn't a big one."

Joe was still clinging to the cable for his life. He couldn't kick out far enough to get his feet on the cavern floor, but no one seemed to notice until the foreman said something about sending Barton up for emergency medical attention.

Then he saw Joe. "Moss, you're hanging on that cable. Don't you know that it might start up at any minute and drag you into a hoisting wheel? It would slice off your hands clean as a lump of lard, it would."

"Dammit, help me get my feet back onto the ground!" Joe bellowed, fearing the dark, seemingly bottomless hole below.

The foreman and another brave miner learned far out over the shaft, and managed to grab and haul Joe back to solid footing.

"You should have jumped on the ore cart like the rest of us," the foreman said.

"I would have, but it looked sort of crowded," Joe answered. "And I wasn't sure how much of that scalding water was going to come rushing into this work station."

"So," the man said, with a wry half smile. "Were you gonna start shimmying eight hundred feet up that cable like a damned monkey?"

"I would have if that was my only choice."

The foreman laughed until he happened to turn and put his candle light on Barton, whose face and chest were blood-red. He knelt beside the suffering Englishman and said, "You got burned real bad. I'm afraid that your skin is going to slough off and you'll carry the scars of this day for the rest of your life."

"But will I live?" Barton sobbed, obviously in severe pain.

"I don't know," the foreman said honestly. "But we'll get you up on top and see what can be done. Good luck."

The cage was finally raised to their eight-hundred-foot level. Several other miners from deeper levels who were already scalded by the cascade of boiling water managed to get Barton squeezed in among them.

"Will he make it?" Joe asked, wanting the truth.

The foreman shook his head. "Usually, when they are burned this bad, their skin sloughs off and they get terrible infections and soon die. And my guess is that the first time that Barton looks in the mirror, he'll pray to die."

Joe understood. And he also understood that he wasn't coming back down into this mine or any other Comstock mine. He'd gotten a taste of it, and it was every bit as hot and hellish as he'd expected.

It was time to go back to the sky and the clean air. And once on top again, that was where he would remain until the day of his death.

25

On a cloudless and bright Sunday morning, Joe rested in the rocking chair and vividly recounted to Beth, Dan DeQuille, Dr. Taylor, and Ellen his harrowing experiences and the hardships of working on the eight-hundred-foot level of the Belcher Mine. A short while later, Dr. Taylor surprised Joe by taking Ellen Johnson on a carriage ride down to Lake's Crossing for shopping. There was room enough for all of them in the doctor's two-horse carriage, but the newspaperman and Beth said they'd rather stay and relax on the veranda.

"I'm going to saddle up Jasper and take him for a ride," Joe announced mainly to Beth. "All of our horses are needing some exercise, but your Jasper seems the most rambunctious."

"He hasn't been ridden for nearly two years," Beth said, looking a little worried. "I'm sure he'd love to get out and gallop."

Joe doubted that, but he was curious about the big bay gelding, and so he headed off to get the animal saddled and bridled. DeQuille and Beth, meanwhile, had remained talking on the porch, and Joe wondered if they were going to become a pair. They were well matched in interests, education, and intellect and could chatter for hours about books and poets. Dan DeQuille was a handsome and articulate man, but Joe guessed they didn't pay much money at the newspapers because, although DeQuille tried to keep up appearances, his clothes were shiny with wear and his heels were worn down to nothing. He also was in real need of a barbershop shave and haircut.

And what about Dr. Taylor and Ellen? Joe couldn't help but feel a little jealous about how they were getting on so well. This told him that he was emotionally attached to the ex-Mormon farm woman more than he'd realized. But he also was happy for Ellen because she deserved an educated and professional man, not some rough-and-ready fella like Joe Moss who barely had enough manners to sit at the table in good company. Besides, the doctor was a fine man who had never married, yet seemed interested in trying to become a good husband and father.

So that Sunday morning as the two pairs enjoyed each other's company, Joe thought he might saddle up that jug-headed Jasper and ride the big old horse down to St. Mary of the Mountain Church and perhaps be rewarded by the sight of Jessica. He hungered just for a quick look at his beautiful daughter.

"Whoa, Jasper!" Joe yelled, trying to force the bit between the animal's long yellow teeth. "Cooperate, you ugly beast!"

In response, Jasper tossed his muzzle high into the air, so high that even Joe couldn't stand on his toes and get the bit set. Angry now, Joe reared back and kicked Jasper hard in his bulging hay belly. Now that got the animal's full attention! In fact, Jasper tried to bite Joe on the arm, and instead ripped the sleeve off one of his new shirts. They went around and around fighting each other's will until Joe finally eared the brute and bitted it fair. Then he cinched down his saddle and swung on board.

Jasper charged out of the little corral, splintering two rails and a cedar post. He shot around the mansion and went flying down the hill into town with Joe holding onto the saddle horn for dear life. He heard the doctor and Beth shouting at him, but Joe was moving so fast that he couldn't hear their words. Down the mountainside they barreled straight through an intersection past C Street and on down the hill at full bore.

Several people were almost trampled, and Joe was hauling back on the reins for all he was worth, yet Jasper had the bit firmly between his teeth and his great thick neck defied all of Joe's considerable strength.

They sailed past the Catholic church, and Joe caught a momentary glimpse of little Jessica playing, yet hardly had time to wave. Jasper hit the bottom of a rocky ravine, lost his footing, and tumbled, throwing Joe hard into the brush. Momentarily stunned, Joe staggered erect to see that Jasper was tangled in the brush and his reins.

"You miserable jug-head!" Joe shouted, kicking the animal in the rump and then hopping back into the saddle as the priest and nuns watched in shock and amazement.

Jasper was breathing hard, yet still game to run. After all, he had been penned for two years and sensed sweet freedom at last. The slope was still steeply tilted downward when they skidded into the poor people's cemetery, where there were no monuments or even headstones. Jasper trampled over a dozen or more graves and knocked wooden crosses flying, then flattened a rickety wooden fence and kept on running.

"Whoo-ha!" Joe hollered, yanking off his Stetson and batting the old bay across the butt again and again. "Whoo-ha!"

Jasper finally ran out of steam about four miles out into the barren hills. He staggered to a halt and stood with his head held low to the sage and his nostrils distended as he tried to find his wind. But Joe didn't let him rest more than a minute, and then he forced the old fella back into a disjointed gallop. They circled the town, and when they came trotting down from the high side of Mount Davidson, Jasper was moving as smooth and easy as a sore-footed milking cow.

"Joe!" Beth cried from the veranda. "What on earth happened to you and my Jasper!"

Joe Moss tossed his Stetson right up on the porch, and it landed in his favorite rocking chair. "Why, Miss Beth, we're just enjoin' a nice Sunday morning horseback ride. And I even got to briefly pay my respects to the Catholics and little Jessica! I had a *fine* time. Most fun I've had in a long while."

"But look at poor Jasper!" she cried, hands flying to her mouth.

"Why, what's wrong with him?" Joe asked, trying to look innocent.

"He's all covered with white foam and

stickers and dirt. Did he fall, Joe?"

"He just got tired for a minute and laid down kinda sudden to rest," Joe explained. "Nothing to worry about, Beth. Nothing at all!"

Joe started riding Jasper every other day and their other horses in between. He rode everywhere hard and for long hours. He rode back down to Devil's Gate just hoping that fella that had forced him and everyone else to pay a steep toll was alone without his rifleman to back up his play, but he was disappointed to see nothing had changed. No matter, the time would come for a reckoning.

Joe also rode his Palouse down Geiger Grade toward Lake's Crossing and then all the way back. It was a long, steep ride, but he talked to a lot of freighters and had a pretty good time. What he needed and wanted was his Fiona and his daughter, but at least he was out again in the fresh air under the bright, blue Nevada sky, and just doing that made him think that somehow everything was going to work out for the best.

"Joe," Ellen said late one afternoon, "Dr. Taylor has asked me to go work in his office. He needs help and as you know, I am good nursing the sick and injured. I think that I'll take him up on his offer."

"Fine idea," Joe agreed. "But I'll miss having you around during the day."

"What are *you* going to do, Joe? You're riding our horses down to skin and bones."

Joe had been thinking about it on those long rides all over these barren hills, and thought he had a sensible answer to her question. "I'm going to track down the Peabody family and tell them that Fiona couldn't have murdered Mr. Peabody."

"I don't think they'll believe you since you weren't even on the Comstock Lode when Chester Peabody was stabbed to death that night."

"That may be true," Joe replied. "But I want to hear their account of the killing, and then maybe I can decide what I need to do to find Fiona."

Ellen didn't seem to think that was a good idea, but she knew Joe well enough not to argue the point with him, so she just started talking about how good it would be to work for a real doctor and how much she could learn and how it would be nice to have some income.

Joe nodded his head, but he really wasn't listening. It was obvious that Ellen was going to work mostly so she could be near Dr.

Taylor. Even a blind man could see that the pair were in love and would eventually get married. That was good for them, and Joe was happy for the couple because they were fine people who deserved some real happiness.

As for himself, he would never be happy until he found Fiona and was able to reclaim his daughter. And given that, he need to track down the Peabody men and see if they had retribution in mind for his Fiona.

Because if they did . . . well, maybe he'd have to kill and scalp one or two of them.

26

Dan Dequille had already informed Joe all about the Peabody family. They owned and operated one of the richest mines on the Comstock Lode located just over The Divide that separated the rival towns of Gold Hill from Virginia City. It was called the Shamrock Mine, even though the Peabody family was proud to be known as Englishmen.

"They got very lucky early," DeQuille had explained. "And their mine is one of the few where the mother lode rises almost to the surface, so their costs of extraction are much lower than the deep mines we have working far below Virginia City. The Peabody family is very clannish, very prominent, arrogant, and overbearing as Englishmen often tend to be."

"How many men left in that family?" Joe asked.

"Chester J. Peabody was the patriarch,

their leader. But he is survived by three brothers who have large families. The Shamrock Mine makes no bones about the fact that they prefer to hire English, Scottish, and Welsh men . . . no Irish need apply. They are a tough bunch, Joe. Tough, rich, and said to be ruthless despite their well-cultivated air of being generous benefactors to local charities."

Joe had taken all that family background in, and now he was riding his Palouse horse over The Divide and down toward the Shamrock Mine just a little ways above Gold Hill. When he arrived at the mine property, the very first thing he noticed was that there weren't the usual monstrous tin buildings that housed hoisting works. Instead, there were five or six smaller tin buildings and an immense mound of mine tailings. Ore wagons were being loaded by a dozen or so workmen, who stood on a high abutment and shoveled ore down into the waiting wagons from both sides.

The entire mining operation was circled by a ten-strand barbed-wire fence, and there were NO TRESPASSING signs posted every five or six feet. All in all, Joe had the feeling that this was not a very hospitable place and it didn't like strangers.

An armed guard stopped Joe at the only

gate in and out of the rich claim, and demanded to know what business Joe had at the Shamrock Mine.

"I've come to see the Peabody men," Joe informed him, rankled because the guard pointed his rifle in Joe's direction.

"They ain't hirin'," the guard said, looking happy about the fact. "So you might as well turn that spotted horse around and ride back to wherever it is that you started from today."

Joe could see that this man was about the same sort of hostile sonofabitch that the fella at Devil's Gate had been. Unfriendly and downright insulting.

"Well," Joe said, stepping down from his horse and leading it up close to the guard, "I wasn't exactly lookin' for work."

"Then what do you want here?"

Joe smiled and used his thumb to tip his hat back so the sun was full on his rugged face. "Actually, what I want most of all right now is to slap that sneer off your pug-ugly face."

"Huh?"

Joe Moss backhanded the guard so hard that the man staggered and then tripped and landed against the barbed-wire fence. He let out a scream as the barbs tore his flesh. Joe stepped forward and hit him with a thundering uppercut to the jaw that knocked him completely over the top strand of wire and out cold on the ground.

"I don't know what it is about you fellas that are guards in this neck of the woods," Joe said, leading his horse through the gate and collecting the guard's weapons, "but you all seem to be stamped out of the same disagreeable mold."

Joe remounted his horse and rode onto the mine property. He expected that he had already made a mighty poor impression, but he was operating on a short tether and would brook no sass or disrespect today. Not even from the Peabody men, who thought themselves to be the cocks of the walk.

He dismounted by a shack after slowly reading the words: SHAMROCK MINE HEADQUARTERS . . . ONLY THOSE INVITED CAN ENTER.

"Well," he said to his horse as he tied the animal up in front of the headquarters, "let's see if we can get along a little better with management."

When he entered the office, he saw a lot of desks, most of which had more ore samples than papers on them, and at least six or seven busy men. They all turned to stare at Joe, and finally one of them detached from the rest and came over to confront Joe. This man, with a white shirt, coat, and black tie, was about five feet eleven and two hundred pounds, and he bore the look of what Joe would have expected of an aristocratic Englishman.

"Who are you and what do you want?"

Joe stuck out his hand, but it was ignored, so he dropped it to his side and replied, "My name is Joe Moss. I have some business to discuss with the Peabody men about my wife, Fiona Moss."

Joe's words were loud and clear, and it stopped the activity in the office like a clock that suddenly came unwound. The man in front of Joe stepped back a pace, and visibly stiffened like an English bulldog meeting another fighting dog. Two other large men came hurrying across the office to stand beside him.

"You must be the three survivin' Peabody brothers," Joe said, hands not far from his gun on one hip and tomahawk on the other. "First off, I came to introduce myself. Fiona and I never got formally hitched, but we are married in the way that Indians marry, and that is in the union of body and *spirit*. And second off, that is my daughter that the priest and the nuns are carin' for at St. Mary of the Mountain and I aim to get her back one way or another."

"Joe Moss, what the hell are you here for?" the biggest of the brothers hissed. "Are you just plain too ignorant to know that your woman murdered our oldest brother?"

The rest of the men in the office building were now marching over to stand behind the Peabody brothers, and there wasn't a single friendly face among them. Joe was starting to feel crowded and cornered.

He gave the Peabody brothers one more chance to see the light. "I'm here to tell you that Fiona *couldn't* have murdered your oldest brother."

"You were *there*, Joe Moss?"

"No, sir, I was not. But —"

"Gawdamn! You must be dumber than dirt," one of the brothers hissed. " 'Cause that's the only explanation why you'd tell us this bullshit when you weren't even present when that bloody bitch stabbed our older brother to death. Stabbed him in the back six times, the doctor said, when they laid poor Chester out on the slab!"

Joe's hands knotted into fists and he felt a raging fire starting to burn way down in his gut. "Out of respect for your loss I am goin' to forgive what you just called my Fiona," Joe breathed, words coming very hard and slow. "But the thing I want to tell you is

286

that Fiona wouldn't hurt a fly."

"You're dead wrong, Moss," one of them growled. "And when our bounty hunter, Ike Grady, hunts her down and drags what's left of her carcass back to Virginia City to be tried for murder and hanged, you'll see how wrong you are about that *bitch!*"

Joe had forgiven the slur word one time, but he damn sure wasn't of a mind to forgive it a second time. Without word or warning, he hit that lying Peabody right between the eyes with every ounce of his coiled fury and muscle. Peabody went down like a felled pine, and Joe would have kicked him in the head, except the other two brothers along with everybody else in the room came down on him like a rock slide. Next thing he knew he was buried and being beaten worse than the orneriest mule.

Joe fought with his teeth, his hands, and his feet, but he had no chance at all. They seemed to take special delight in kicking him in the crotch and trying to pound his nose through the back of his head. He lost consciousness and when he awoke, he was tied across the Palouse horse and it was galloping over The Divide and then heading for its barn.

He didn't see Ellen and Beth or hear them screaming when the horse trotted along in front of the veranda carrying what looked more like a side of butchered beef than a human being.

And maybe that was just as well because Joe didn't want to come back to the Comstock Lode and its meanness for a good long while.

27

It took nearly two months for Joe to recover from his terrible beating, and even then he wasn't feeling in the best of health when he saddled the Palouse and headed off one evening to visit the Shamrock Mine. Because the Shamrock was a surface dig where the ore came out of a huge hole in the ground, it did not operate a twenty-four-hour shift, but was shut down between six o'clock in the evening and six o'clock in the morning.

Joe arrived at eight o'clock when the sun was down and before the stars came out. He tied his horse out behind a mountainous tailing where it could not be seen or struck by flying debris. From his saddlebags, he removed three sticks of dynamite that he'd bought from a mining supply company, then ignored the heavy gate and cut the barbed-wire fence. He limped over to the silent headquarters office. It was locked up tight.

"Only those invited can enter, huh?" Joe said, again reading the big, unfriendly sign. "Well, that's fine and dandy 'cause I do not *need* to enter."

Joe found a rock, wrapped it in a bandanna, and smashed the front office window. Humming a tune, he casually lit the first stick of dynamite . . . the one with a very, very long fuse. He tossed the stick into the headquarters office, then limped over to another big building and did the same with a slightly shorter fuse. Finally, he came to a giant workshop where at least five big ore wagons were in various stages of repair. Joe pitched the third stick of dynamite in among those wagons, then limped back to his horse.

He had time to untie the animal and climb into the saddle before the first stick of dynamite shook every structure in Gold Hill and rattled windows for a mile in all directions. The spotted horse took off running, and Joe just let the animal race over the hills as the second and third sticks of dynamite obliterated the entire Shamrock Mining operation. A cloud of rock and dust sprouted like a giant mushroom and rose hundreds of feet into the night sky.

High up on Mount Davidson, or Sun Mountain as many preferred to call it, Joe rested his horse and gazed down at the inferno that was already feeding up into the swirling dust storm. He could faintly hear shouting, and knew that the Gold Hill Voluntary Fire Department would be way too little and way too late.

"Peabody men . . . I reckon this will keep your minds off doing harm to my Fiona at least for the next few months," he said to himself. "Plenty long enough for me to track down your hired bounty hunter and give that pilgrim a whole new outlook on life . . . or send him along to the Promised Land."

Joe smiled with satisfaction, then rode down the western slope of the mountain into the green Washoe Valley, where there was a lake fed by a stream from the Sierras that was a sight for his sore eyes. It was about one o'clock in the morning and he was tired, so he hobbled his horse, spread a bedroll, and slept until the sun came up and made the snowcapped peaks to the west shine like diamonds. There were fish jumping in the shallow lake and, Lord, but he'd have enjoyed skinnin' a stick and trying to rig a hook and line. He hadn't had fresh trout in way too long.

"I'm goin' back to the high mountains

where the cold water flows when this is all done," he promised himself as he admired the Sierras, then rolled his blankets and prepared to move along.

While convalescing, Joe Moss had learned a thing or two about the bounty hunter named Ike Grady. Learned that the man had once been a United States marshal and then a Pinkerton Agency detective. Learned that Grady was corrupt and had been fired from both positions, but also that he was a crack shot and fearless.

Joe wasn't worried because he was as good with a rifle as he was with a knife and his tomahawk. His weakness, he knew, was with a six-gun. He'd just never liked them much, and his hands and fingers were too big and stiff after years of working with animals and trapping beaver in icy streams.

"I probably should have bought me a double-barreled shotgun," he said to himself as he watched the Palouse greedily feed on grass, something that it had not enjoyed since it had arrived on the Comstock Lode and been put on a steady diet of cured hay.

Joe could only imagine what was going on in Gold Hill after what he suspected would be the almost complete destruction of the Shamrock Mine. At this point, he doubted that he would be a suspect in the dynamiting because two months had passed since his fateful visit. But when the Peabody Englishmen learned that their hired gunman had suddenly vanished, or had had a major change of heart in terms of his line of work, they would probably figure it out. However, by then, they would have no proof of Joe's involvement, just like they really had no proof that it had been Fiona who had stabbed their brother to death.

"It's all circumstantial," Joe muttered, going off to bridle and then saddle his horse. "At least, that's the word I seem to remember Dan DeQuille using when people are sure of a fact without really being able to prove it."

Joe saddled the horse, mounted, and rode on toward Lake's Crossing, where Ike Grady was said to be living on the north end of town. The man was said to have a little ranch called the Circle G resting on a couple of hundred acres of rock and brush. Joe chewed Beth Hamilton's good sourdough biscuits as he rode along admiring the scenery, and when he came to Lake's Crossing, he made a point to circle around the town and then continued steadily north.

It was well after dark, only twenty-four hours since he'd paid an unexpected call on the Shamrock Mine, when he arrived at a ranch gate that had a circle G brand burned into the wood.

Joe could see the lights of a shack about a quarter mile ahead. He cut Grady's fence with the same wire snips he'd used on the Shamrock Mine's barbed wire, and then remounted and rode up the ruts toward the lonely farmhouse. He had one more stick of dynamite in his saddlebags, but he knew that he couldn't use it for fear that Ike Grady had a woman or kids living in his run-down shack.

Joe checked his rifle and pistol, his bowie knife and tomahawk. A huge dog started barking, and he knew that his arrival would be noticed by Ike.

"Hello the house?" Joe called.

The lights in the windows dimmed low. No one appeared, and the dog was coming toward him. By the size of its silhouette, he could see that it was almost as big as a wolf and it was making one hell of a loud racket. Joe did his best to ignore the beast, hoping it wouldn't try to bite his horse's legs.

"Hello the house! Ike Grady? I got a message from Mr. Peabody!"

Joe saw a dark form appear partially hidden in the doorway. "Who are you and why the hell you comin' around this time of the damned night?"

"It's about that Moss woman!"

There was a long silence, and then Ike took the bait. "What about her?"

"She. . . ." Joe didn't know why he said what he said next, but it just came out, so he let it hang in the air. "She's hiding in Carson City, but she's said to have been shot and might even be dyin'."

Ike digested this bit of news and swore bitterly. "Dammit, *I'm* the one that's being paid to shoot her! Who did it?"

"Well," Joe said, slipping his sidearm out of his holster and into his coat pocket, "that's what Mr. Peabody sent me to tell you all about."

"Shit!" Ike cursed. "Dog, shut up or I'll put a damned bullet in you!"

The dog, hearing the anger in its master's voice, turned and trotted back to the shack. Ike was furious because he probably was thinking about all the money he wasn't going to make by either capturing or killing Fiona. So he kicked at the huge dog, and it jumped back untouched and snarling. Joe liked that because it showed the dog had some sand in his craw and would not be abused without putting up a fight.

"You want to know about that wounded Moss woman or not?" Joe called.

"Come on in, mister, but keep those

hands on your saddle horn."

Joe rode right up to the shack and dismounted without an invitation. Ike was holding a double-barreled shotgun and it was pointed in Joe's direction. And Joe knew that the man would not hesitate to kill him.

"Why you comin' out so late?" Ike asked.

" 'Cause they sent me over here from the Shamrock first thing this morning and told me to ride hard. Mister, I'm tired, hungry, and most of all thirsty. You got any food or whiskey?"

"I do if you got money," Ike said, lowering the shotgun.

"I do."

"Then come inside and sit at the table," Ike groused, "but damned if I like the news you've brought."

"I didn't expect you would," Joe told the man as he entered the cabin, which was filthy and stank so bad it nearly took his breath away. Any thought of being hungry vanished from Joe's head at that moment.

"Sit down! I got some old salt pork and beans. But first, let's see the color of your money."

Joe laid two dollars on the rough-hewn table and Ike snatched it up saying, "You kin sleep tonight in the shed out back."

"Whiskey," Joe said impatiently. "I ain't

payin' two whole dollars for just salt pork and beans."

"What the hell happened to your face, mister?" Ike asked, squinting in the candle light. "You sure did take a beating from someone. They whipped your ass real good, didn't they!"

"Yeah, they did. About ten of 'em," Joe said as Ike Grady brought out a jug and filled two cracked glasses with home brew. "But I'm mending."

"You'll bear the scars to your grave," Ike told him, raising his glass. "I could see that you were limpin' a mite as well. But what I want to know is how that Moss woman got herself shot in Carson City."

"How much money are you out from the Peabody family if she dies?" Joe asked quietly, raising his own glass, then taking a swallow that tasted like turpentine.

"Three hundred dollars," Ike said, angry. "And I really need that damned money!"

Joe looked around and thought about how worthless this land up here was for anything useful. "Yeah, Ike," he said, "I can see that you do. Don't you have anyone else to capture or kill for a bounty?"

"Not at the moment," Ike Grady admitted. "I put all the time I got to spare tryin' to find that damned Moss woman. Heard a rumor that she went to California. So damned if I didn't go all the way to San Francisco lookin' for her murderin' hide. But she wasn't there. Nope. I asked practically everyone in the city that might know, and then I rode a stagecoach all the way down to Old Monterey 'cause someone told me she'd gone there instead. But she didn't. Didn't go to Sacramento, either."

Ike was getting angrier and angrier just in telling Joe about the futility of his hunt. "So I came back here, and then got another rumor that Fiona Moss was hidin' out east of town where a bunch of Paiute Indians live. I figured that was a good hiding place, so I went out there and gave the chief blood money. Gave all of 'em some money, but those Paiutes played me like a fish on a line. Took me a week and about fifty dollars before I was sure that them damned bug-eaters didn't know Fiona Moss and had never even heard of her before I came along."

"Sounds like it ain't been easy," Joe commiserated. "What about that big dog of yours?"

"What about him?" Ike demanded.

"Do you take him along or does he fend out here in this sagebrush country for himself?"

"I ain't *never* fed a dog. They either make it on their own or they starve. But that dog, he's half wolf and he'll kill other dogs if they growl at him. Kill deer, rabbits, and even antelope, too. Coyotes? Well, he just runs them down and has 'em for dessert."

"Sounds like quite a dog," Joe said, genuinely impressed. "I once had a big dog that was kind of like that. He didn't like many people."

"Well, this dog don't like many people, either."

"Including you," Joe said.

Ike managed a sheepish grin. "No, he don't like me, either. There was an old man that used to work for me here and he brought the dog onto this ranch. Then the old man got roaring drunk one night and tried to collect his back pay, so I paid him in lead. Savvy?"

"I savvy."

"His dog tried to tear out my throat when I hauled the old man's carcass out into the back and buried it in the sand. The dog stayed around to be near that grave and he just never went away."

"What did the old man call the dog?"

"Rip." Ike shook his head. "Can you believe a man who would name a dog Rip?"

"Sounds like a good name to me," Joe

said. "RIP. Maybe it stands for Rest In Peace . . . like you've seen on so many gravestones."

"Huh? Never thought of that. Maybe so. Anyway, that's what the old man is doin' right now out behind my cabin! He's RIP for sure!"

Ike Grady thought that was awfully funny and began to laugh. Joe went cold inside and said, "So Ike, what will you do now that Fiona Moss is shot and laid up in Carson City?"

"Why, I'll hightail it down there and make sure that I can lay claim to finishin' the job."

Joe took another drink. "So you'll find and kill her?"

"Sure! What difference is it to me if she's already shot and half-dead? As long as I get that three hundred dollars from the Peabody family, then I'm a happy man."

"That's kind of what I thought you'd say," Joe said.

"For three hundred dollars I'd kill the President of the United States!"

Joe scratched at a scab on his hand. "I expect you would . . . if you could."

"Oh, I could all right!" Ike Grady bragged as he poured them both another glass. "I can shoot the head off a sparrow on the wing. Never miss."

"Killed a lot of men, have you, Ike?"

"More'n I remember," Grady bragged. "And by the way, why do you carry a damned tomahawk in your belt? You ain't no stinkin' Injun."

Joe drained his glass, feeling the liquid fire spread. He pulled the tomahawk out of his belt and gently laid it on the table so that Ike Grady could see the weapon. "Oh, I'm Injun all right," Joe told the bounty hunter. "But not a Paiute. I'm more like a Blackfoot or a Sioux."

"I never killed one of them," Grady said, fingering the heavy and very sharp blade of the tomahawk. "I never even took a scalp."

"And you never will," Joe said softly.

"Huh?"

In a smooth, sweeping motion Joe grabbed the tomahawk and struck Ike Grady just below his jaw, nearly beheading the bounty hunter. Grady's blood spewed across the table and the man's eyes bulged. He was still shaking and choking when Joe calmly went around the table and then scalped him with practiced precision.

"I guess I'll drink the rest of that jug out in your shed. Don't much like the smell of things in here," Joe told the still-quivering corpse.

Outside, Rip was waiting with his ruff

301

standing on end and his fangs white in the moonlight. Joe listened to the rumbling in the huge beast's throat, and he turned around and went back into the cabin. Moments later, he returned to the door with a hunk of salt pork and tossed it to the beast.

"I'd feed you sometimes if you wanted to come along with me," he told Rip. "Think about it for a day or two and then decide if you want to leave this land with me or not."

Joe sidestepped the dog, which was devouring the pork. He went and unsaddled his horse, and found some grain in the shed and some half-moldy hay along with a small burro. There was a pack for the burro and some gold-panning equipment tossed in a heap.

"I guess Ike was a prospector as well as a hired killer," Joe said to himself as he unrolled his blankets and spread them out on the straw.

"You can come back to us now, Fiona," Joe said with a yawn as he stretched out on his blankets. "I took care of everything that was going to hurt you and now it's all safe and fine. Me and little Jessica are going to be waiting for you in Virginia City."

And then Joe drifted off into the best sleep he'd had since almost being beaten to death at the former Shamrock Mine.

28

Joe camped at Ike Grady's little homestead ranch a few days just to observe the big wolf-dog named Rip. It was clear that the animal had been neglected all its life, but Joe admired his spirit, size, and independence. Mostly, he wanted to know if Rip could be ever trusted and be a good dog for him.

The day after the killing, Joe buried Ike Grady out near another burial mound that he guessed was that of the old man that had once owned and perhaps even loved Rip. The big dog watched Joe carefully as he buried Ike, and then the animal sat beside the grave of his former owner and howled mournfully all day.

"You loved the old man, didn't you," Joe said that evening when he went out to feed Rip some salt pork. "I admire your independence and I admire your loyalty. Maybe you'd like to be friends. I'd treat you well;

feed you when you weren't able to hunt. In return, you'd be my watchdog and side-kick."

Rip cocked his massive head sideways, listening intently as Joe continued. " 'Cause you see, what might happen is that this bunch called the Peabody family is probably gonna figure out that I'm the one that not only blew up their mine and equipment, but also shot their hired killer. And when they come to that conclusion, they're gonna want me dead real bad. Maybe they'd even want to skin me alive and make me suffer for a while, for I did a powerful amount of damage to them with those sticks of dynamite."

Joe used his bowie to cut off a chunk of salt pork, which he tossed to the ravenous dog. "Understand my problem?"

Rip devoured the meat, then listened, licking his chops.

"Good," Joe said. "I had a hunch you were smart. And with a dog like you, I would have a far better chance of being warned when those Peabody fellas or someone they hired come to kill me. So what I'm sayin', Big Dog, is that we could be real useful to each other."

Joe finished burying Ike Grady and wiped

the sweat from his brow. He gazed out toward the low, barren hills and watched a dust devil dance in the heat. He saw a turkey vulture soaring on the rising hot hair looking for something . . . anything already dead to eat. Damned if this wasn't the most gawd-awful country Joe had ever seen.

"Rip, I've got a woman named Fiona who is also in a lot of trouble hiding somewhere. And we have a pretty little girl. Tomorrow I'm gonna burn down Ike's stinkin' ranch shack and set his burro free because it can make it in this country, if the Indians don't catch and eat him. Now, Dog, you can tag along with the burro or you can follow along with me; the choice is purely your own. My feelin' has always been that a worthy dog has to make up its own mind about who it likes or doesn't like."

Joe saw a handkerchief lying half-buried in the dirt not far away. He noticed that Rip was lying near it, and he suspected that the handkerchief had belonged to the old man and that it was the last thing that the dog had to remind it of his former friend. "Rip, how about I take that handkerchief and wear it a while?"

But when Joe tried to retrieve the handkerchief, Rip growled, bared his teeth, and would not let Joe near the handkerchief.

"All right," Joe said, raising his hands and backing away. "It's yours . . . for the time being."

Later that day, however, when Rip went off on a hunting foray, Joe collected the dirty, bloodstained handkerchief and instead of washing it, he just tied it loosely around his neck. Rip returned a few hours later with blood on his muzzle and a half-eaten rabbit in his jaws. He sat down in front of the shack and finished the rabbit, then watched Joe closely for a while.

"Yep, I am wearin' the old man's handkerchief," Joe confessed to the wary beast. "I sure hope you're not of a mind to grab me by the throat and take it back."

Rip watched Joe all the rest of that day and never let him go out of sight. That night he slept not far from Joe in the barn, and followed him about the next morning when he fed the horses and burro and then went back into the cabin and collected anything of value in a small sack. Other than a pistol and rifle that were even better than his own weapons, Ike Grady hadn't anything worth taking.

"I sure can see why Ike needed that three hundred dollars in bounty for killin' my Fiona," Joe said to the dog. "I wouldn't give you a silver dollar for this whole ugly ranch."

Rip sat in the shade of a mesquite and listened as Joe talked, and then Joe set a match to the shack. The place went up in a hurry with flames lifting fifty feet into the blue sky.

"I'm fixin' to head back to Virginia City today," Joe told the dog as he saddled his horse. "And like I said . . . you can come along and we'll watch out for each other . . . or you can stay out here and kill rabbits and coyotes until you finally get so old and slow that the coyotes kill and eat *you*. So what's it to be?"

The big dog padded over to the grave and lay down beside where the old man rested.

"I accept your choice," Joe said. "Good hunting."

He reined his Palouse horse south toward Lake's Crossing and the Comstock Lode, satisfied that he'd done the right thing by killing Ike Grady before he'd had his chance at Fiona.

But where was Fiona now? That was the question that was slowly driving Joe crazy. The only thing he was sure of was that Fiona would eventually return to Virginia City to claim their beautiful daughter. And when she did, he'd be there and they'd be reunited and go off someplace where the cool pines sang in the breeze and the cold streams made a person feel like they were drinking the elixir of life.

Joe heard pounding feet, then a moment later the thin, terrified shriek of a dying jackrabbit. He twisted around in his saddle and saw Rip galloping through the sage with another furry meal in his mouth as he fell in behind the Palouse horse, chewing and swallowing on the move.

A big grin creased Joe's battered and still-swollen face and he said, "Glad you decided to tag along, Rip! We're going to make a good team, you and me. And before we're done with our time, I'll show you country so green and pretty that this ugly high desert will be nothin' more'n a bad memory for either of us in our old age."

Rip looked up at him with the dead rabbit dangling in his great jaws. Joe held his horse up for a minute while the dog made the rabbit disappear. A few miles back, a small cloud of smoke hung in the sky, and Joe knew it was all that was left of the Circle G Ranch.

"Let's go, Dog. I sure hope you can abide livin' in Virginia City with all its people until Fiona comes back and we can leave. And you've got to promise me that you won't go around killin' and eatin' all the town dogs."

In reply, Rip licked his bloody chops and

followed his new master south toward
Lake's Crossing and the Comstock Lode.

29

When Joe rode up C Street with giant Rip trotting along behind his horse, their appearance created quite a stir. The usual collection of town dogs that challenged intruders bold enough to enter their territory simply looked at mighty Rip and immediately headed off to find other distractions, or ducked under the boardwalk to hide.

Joe drew rein at Mrs. Hamilton's mansion and dismounted before leading his weary horse around behind to the stable. Jasper made a big fuss over their arrival, and Rip lifted his leg and began to mark his territory around the barn and mansion.

"You'd best not piss all over Beth's roses," Joe warned the beast. "For she would not take that kindly."

The big dog wagged his tail and set off to do some exploring of the neighborhood. Joe wasn't worried because he knew the dog would not venture off too far and would avoid people.

"Where on earth did you get that *wolf?*" Beth exclaimed.

"He's at least part dog," Joe answered. "And I found him up north."

"We were all hoping that you'd come back here with Fiona, not an animal like that."

"Rip is going to make us a fine watchdog."

"Is he friendly?"

"Not especially," Joe admitted. "But he'll warm to you if you let him do it on his own time schedule. Where is Ellen?"

"She's working for Dr. Taylor every day now."

"Those two seem to have taken a real liking to each other."

"That's quite obvious to anyone," Beth said. "And to think that it was *you* that brought them together. Joe, aren't you going to tell me what happened while you were gone?"

Joe unsaddled and unbridled his tired spotted horse and turned it loose in its pen. He took his gear into the little barn and poured some grain for the horse. Jasper, as always, tried to bully his way to the grain, but the Palouse bared his teeth and drove Beth's gelding away.

"Horses aren't real good about sharing grain, are they," Beth observed.

311

"Nope," Joe said.

"Well, what happened? Did you find that bounty hunter and talk him into leaving your Fiona alone?"

"I guess you could say that Ike Grady isn't going to hunt down and kill anyone for money ever again."

"That's good to hear," Beth said. "And I'm glad that you were able to make Mr. Grady see a better way."

"Yeah," Joe said, not wanting her to see his face. "He's restin' a lot easier now."

"Do you think he would have actually killed Fiona for the Peabody men?"

"No doubt about that," Joe said. "Ike told me that they were payin' him three hundred dollars."

"That's not very much money in exchange for selling your soul," Beth answered.

"No, it wasn't." Joe needed to change the subject. "Did you find another lawyer that might help me get Jessica back? One that I could afford?"

"I talked to several and they all agree that it won't be easy . . . or cheap."

Joe frowned. "But it can be done?"

"It might be done." Beth frowned. "Joe, one of the lawyers told me that you'd have to grease some big palms in Storey County."

Joe had been expecting it might come

down to paying off a judge and a politician or two. "How much, Beth?"

"Maybe as much as ten thousand dollars. Father O'Connor is very popular and very much opposed to letting Jessica out of his grasp. As you might expect, your daughter has become quite a favorite among the nuns."

"Is the priest also expecting a payoff?"

Beth shook her head. "No. But I wouldn't be surprised if a little extra money did wind up in the collection basket should someone important make the decision that you were Jessica's legal father and guardian."

Joe saw that Beth noticed that he had gained an extra rifle and pistol. He was hoping that she wouldn't ask about the new weapons.

"Beth, I sure am thirsty."

"Then come on up to the house and I'll pour us some of my good whiskey. You look awfully tired."

"It was a long, hard ride," Joe admitted. "But I took care of business and I got myself a dandy big dog. His name, by the way, is Rip."

"Fitting name judging from his fierce appearance. Rip looks like a man-eater to me. I'd be scared to get near that beast."

"He's never going to be a real sociable

dog," Joe admitted. "But if someone comes for me in the night, he's going to be the one that tells us all we have trouble long before we'd have figured it out ourselves."

Joe and Beth adjourned to the veranda and while Joe settled into his favorite rocking chair, Beth brought them both glasses of whiskey.

"Joe, I went down and saw Jessica while you were gone."

He looked sideways at her. "That's nice. Did you talk to her some?"

"I did."

Joe took a sip. "What did she say about her mother?"

Beth took a drink and stared out across the Comstock. "She says that her mother promised her that she wouldn't stay away long. That she'd come and get her as soon as she could and then they would go away to someplace real nice."

"That's good to hear, Beth. Did Fiona tell the child where she was going?"

Beth swallowed half her glass of whiskey. "As a matter of fact, she did."

"Where, Beth? Where did she tell the child she was going?"

"To stay with friends in Lake's Crossing."

Joe's hand tightened on his glass. "And did she tell you the name of those friends?"

Beth shook her head. "But I might be able to guess."

Joe waited until Beth said, "There was a couple that lived up here in Virginia City for about six months. The woman became very close friends with Fiona. Then she got quite ill and Dr. Taylor said that it was probably the bad water up here that was causing her so much stomach pain. She and her husband left here to live in Lake's Crossing. The husband is a gifted photographer despite the fact that he has poor eyesight. Before the man left, he took a lot of photographs deep down in the mines. Said he wanted to show the entire world what it was like working a thousand feet underground on the Comstock Lode. Especially the cramped tunnels and the dangerous conditions. He planned to sell them to newspapers and magazines and perhaps put them in a bound collection."

"What's the husband's full name?" Joe demanded, trying to keep his voice calm.

"His name was unusual. It was Faxon Roderus. He told me once that Faxon was Teutonic . . . German . . . and it meant 'long hair.' "

Joe was amused. "Did Faxon have long hair?"

"No," Beth said with a giggle, "Faxon was

as bald as a billiard ball."

"With a name like Faxon Roderus, it shouldn't be all that hard to find that family and my Fiona." Joe started to rise to his feet.

"Where are you going?"

"To Lake's Crossing. Can I borrow Jasper? My horse is plumb worn out."

"So are you, Joe. And I notice that you're still limping. Why don't you stay here for a few days and rest?"

Joe knuckled his eyes. He knew that he still hadn't fully recovered from the savage beating he'd received at the Shamrock Mine and that he looked terrible. He could deal with the exhaustion, but he really didn't want to frighten Fiona by his battered appearance.

"Maybe you're right," he said reluctantly. "I'll wait a few days and then I'll ride my own horse to Lake's Crossing and I'll bring back Fiona."

Beth looked worried. "But what if the Peabody men find out about Ike quitting and decide to wait nearby so that they can hurt her . . . and you? Joe, I realize that you've been through so much trying to find that woman and now that she's close, it's almost impossible to hold back and show prudent caution. But we need to talk about this and

316

think it out clearly because it could mean your *lives*."

Joe tossed his whiskey down, then went into the kitchen and brought out the bottle for them both to share. Beth's glass was empty, so he filled it right along with his own, and they sat and rocked in silence for nearly an hour before Joe said, "I'll wait here for two days before leaving for Lake's Crossing. I'll get a fresh shave and haircut and some more clean clothes. I want to look as good as I can when Fiona sees me again for the first time. It's not that I think she'd love me any less lookin' the way that I do right now, but . . ."

Beth laid a hand on his knee. "I understand. You've been waiting a long time for the day when you meet again, and you're a little afraid that Fiona has changed. That you both have changed. So you want to try and make it come together the best way that you know how."

"She just might not love me anymore, Beth."

"And if she doesn't, what will you do?"

Joe just shook his head. "I can't say. But I have to find out. It's what you don't know that works on your insides."

"Then rest for two days, clean up, and go find that girl," Beth told him. "And when you both return to claim your daughter, then take her and get off the Comstock Lode before the Peabody men have a chance to even know that you were back in town."

"That sounds like mighty good advice," Joe agreed. "But I'd miss you plenty."

"And I'd miss you, Joe Moss. You know, if it hadn't been that you have a daughter and sweetheart, I might have tried to win your heart."

Joe blushed. "The plain truth of it is, Beth, that without even tryin' you halfway did," he confessed, draining his glass, then leaving her to take a much-needed bath.

30

Two days later, Joe rode his horse back down Geiger Grade and up to Lake's Crossing. The town had for years been the emigrants' crossing point over the Truckee River, and had boomed when the hordes of Forty-Niners had resupplied there before making a final assault on the Sierra Nevada Mountains in order to reach the California gold fields. And now, since the discovery of the Comstock Lode, Lake's Crossing was again a major supply point through which most of the heavy machinery and provisions passed.

Unlike Virginia City, Lake's Crossing was a beautiful site located beside the wide and free-flowing Truckee River, which surged down a deep canyon from Lake Tahoe. The south end of Virginia Street bustled with commerce, and Joe had to keep reining his horse off to the side to accommodate the huge freight wagons bound for the Comstock Lode. Not more than twenty feet behind, Rip trotted along with his great head swaying back and forth and his eyes missing nothing.

"Fiona is here," Joe said to his wolf-dog and Palouse horse. "I can feel that Fiona is here and, by gawd, this time I'm gonna find her."

Joe had given the matter of Fiona's disappearance and hiding a great deal of thought. He knew that, by finding her, he was putting her in mortal danger. He also knew that the Peabody men would not rest until she was either hanged or shot. And, in truth, they would do the same to him once they realized he'd blown up their mining company and had killed their bounty hunter, Ike Grady.

"We aren't gonna have much time to get that child at St. Mary's and leave this Nevada Territory," Joe said aloud. "They're gonna be after us and they got enough money to stay after us until we're either dead or I have to kill all of those Peabody men."

Lake's Crossing wasn't nearly as big as Virginia City, but it was sizable and Joe's mind was racing as he rode across the bridge that spanned the Truckee River and tied his horse to a hitching rail.

"Rip, you can stay here with my horse or tag along." Joe's saddlebags held about five pounds of pork and now he fed half of it to the beast. "Just don't be bitin' anybody or chewin' up anybody's dog or cat. I've got my hands full tryin' to find Fiona without havin' to fuss with any extra trouble you might cause."

Rip wolfed down the pork and followed Joe up the street until they came to a gunsmith's shop. Joe stepped inside and said, "Howdy. I'm lookin' for a photographer by the name of Faxon Roderus. I hear he's pretty good."

"You want him to take a picture of you?" the man behind the counter asked, noting Joe's battered but rugged face.

"What if I do?"

The gunsmith glanced down at the beast near Joe and then back at its owner. He forced a wide smile and said, "No offense, sir. You and that dog are . . . are real handsome. And as for Mr. Roderus, he works in his house. That's his studio and darkroom." The man turned and pointed to a framed picture on his wall. "That's me and my wife, Emily. Mr. Roderus took that picture last month. He sure did a fine job."

"That he did," Joe agreed. "Where can I find his house and studio?"

"Just up the street two blocks and turn over one block. He's got a sign out and you can't miss his house."

"Thank you," Joe said, his heart starting to hammer in his chest. "Thank you very much."

"Mister, it's smart to have Faxon take a picture of you and that dog," the man said as Joe was going out the door. "I've never seen anything like him."

"He's different," Joe agreed.

He had no trouble finding the Roderus studio. Faxon had a big sign outside on his lawn advertising his business. It was a nice little wooden house with a picket fence around it and everything was painted yellow. There were flowers in a garden, and it was the kind of a place Fiona would enjoy.

"Well," he said to himself and his new dog, "here we go. If she's here, my heart might just give out on me after so many years."

Joe opened the picket gate and walked up to the door. His knees were knocking and he felt a little weightless even though he was no longer a young man. He knocked on the door, and a voice answered that left no doubt in his mind that it belonged to the love of his life.

"Fiona!"

Joe couldn't contain himself a moment longer. Couldn't wait for his beloved to come to the door and see him after four long years of waiting and wanting. "Fiona!"

He almost tore the door off its hinges as he bounded inside with Rip on his heels. Fiona was coming up the dim hallway. When she saw Joe and the giant dog, she staggered, then fainted dead away.

"Holy shit!" Joe cried. "Maybe her heart gave out from the joy!"

He ran to Fiona's side and gathered her up in his arms. She felt some heavier than he'd remembered . . . or maybe he was some weaker. Didn't matter, really.

"Hey!" a man yelled from the back of the house. "What the . . . what are you doin'!"

Joe was momentarily at a loss for words. "I . . . I . . ."

"Put that woman down!"

"Where?"

Faxon Roderus charged up the hallway. "Give her to me!"

"Not on your life, Mr. Roderus. Get a doctor!"

"Bring her in here," the man said, rushing off with Joe on his heels. "Lay her on that couch. What did you do to her!"

Before Joe could answer, another young woman came running in through the back door and kitchen. Her hands were covered with dirt and Joe knew she had been working in her garden. "What have you done to Fiona!" the young woman screeched.

"Dammit," Joe cried, "I just . . . just showed up to claim her! I think she's just fainted away."

Now both of them spied Rip, who had worked his way down the hall to see what all the commotion was about. The woman's hand flew to her mouth and she screamed. Faxon Roderus jumped for a weapon. Rip growled at his display of aggression as the ruff went up on his back. Roderus found a broom not fit to whip a good-sized cat, but Joe knocked it out of the man's hands.

"Are you folks crazy? I'm Joe Moss! I'm the man that fathered a child with Fiona and has come to marry her and reclaim our daughter Jessica up in Virginia City. Would you folks calm yourselves down a mite and help me see to her?"

"You're Joe Moss," the woman said, staring.

"In the flesh. Now help me with Fiona."

After that, they all spent several frantic minutes trying to revive Fiona. Rip sat down on a rug and glared at the scene as if he blamed Joe for getting him into this excitable mess.

Joe and Fiona were together at last and both still deeply in love. Joe held the only woman he'd ever really loved in his strong arms and nearly cried, telling Fiona about all the troubles he'd had trying to find her, but vowing that it had been well worth it.

Fiona said, "My father forced me to marry that man in California, Joe, thinking he'd get rich off my new husband's claim. But it had been worked out and . . . do you mind if I just don't talk about it now?"

"Nope," Joe said, deciding not to ruin this long-overdue time of joy to tell her that her father was dead. "Fiona, what is done is done. All that counts now is that we're together and we ain't ever going to be parted again. And we're going to go up to Virginia City and get Jessica from the Catholics. But why'd you go and do that to our little Jessica?"

"I was being hunted like a murderess," Fiona confessed. "I had to leave that night that Mr. Peabody was killed or I'd have been lynched. And I knew that I couldn't take our daughter on the run, so I left her at St. Mary's because I was sure that they'd take loving care of her. Joe, I'm sorry!"

He held her close and let her cry it out. "We've both got a lot of talking to do and explaining," Joe said. "I guess we've made some bad mistakes these past four years, and the worst one I ever made was leaving the wagon train without you."

"I *had* to stay," she whispered. "As you well know, I'd given my word to my mother on her deathbed. I just never thought it would be *four years* until I'd see and hold you again."

"I've been hurt pretty bad a few times."

She studied his face. "I can see that, Joe. I can see that you've been hurt very badly. But is your heart still good? Getting hurt didn't turn you mean inside, did it?"

"No," he told her. "But the last beating I got was from the Peabody brothers, and I took revenge on 'em not long ago and blew up their Shamrock Mine with dynamite."

Fiona's eyes widened. "Oh, my heavens! Now they'll want to kill you, too."

"I reckon so," Joe replied, deciding it served no purpose to tell Fiona about the bounty hunter that had been paid to hunt her down for three hundred dollars. "But like I said, what is past is past. Now, we've got to get our daughter and leave this part of the country and go where the Peabody men will never find us."

"Is there such a place, Joe?" she asked, hugging him tightly. "I'm afraid that we'll never rest easy because they won't ever give up."

"There are wild, but safe, hiding places in Montana, the Dakotas, Wyoming, and Colorado where we won't be found. Places where the Indians know and respect me and would not let white bounty hunters track and kill us. So, yes, darlin', I know places where we can go and never even have to worry about our past."

She kissed him on the mouth, and tears were streaming down her pretty cheeks. "Joe, let's go get our daughter and leave Nevada forever."

"That's what we're going to do," Joe promised. "But before we go up there and face that priest and those nuns, I . . . I want us to be married legal."

Fiona cried out with delight. "Oh, Joe, that is what I want too! Let me ask Faxon if he will send for a preacher. We could be married right here in this house within the hour, couldn't we? *Couldn't we?* And Faxon and Milly will stand up for us, Joe!"

"You bet that we could. Have they got a nice bedroom for us to . . . well, you know."

Fiona giggled just like the girl he remembered falling in love with on that wagon train from St. Louis long ago. "Joe, darling, my bedroom has a double bed and it'll serve us well."

They were both blushing when they went out hand in hand to see if Mr. and Mrs. Faxon Roderus would send for a preacher and allow their wedding to be held in their sweet little house and studio.

31

Joe bought Fiona a pretty bay mare and saddle in Lake's Crossing. The sorrel mare was as tall as his Palouse horse and probably faster; he'd paid more for her than he'd ever spent on any two horses.

"You need a fast, strong horse," Joe told her as they rode back up steep Geiger Grade toward Virginia City. "And you also have need of this gun and rifle."

He gave her his own weapons, and kept those that he'd gotten from Ike Grady. "Can you shoot?"

Fiona nodded. "I'm a fair shot with a rifle, not too good with a pistol. But, Joe, I don't want to have to shoot and kill the Peabody men or anyone else."

Joe was itching to ask her about the death of Mr. Chester J. Peabody, but decided that she would explain how her butcher knife had ended up in the prominent man's back when the time to tell was to her liking. Or

329

maybe she'd never be able to talk about it, which was all right with Joe, who had killed dozens of men in his days when they'd needed killing.

"Fiona," he said, "we're hopin' not to have to shoot anybody up on the Comstock Lode, but you have to be ready for whatever trouble comes. Those weapons are loaded and they shoot straight."

Fiona wrapped the gun belt loosely around her waist and pushed Joe's rifle into her scabbard. "I'm so happy now that we're married and together at last that I'm frightened half to death something is about to go terribly wrong."

"I've got the same worry," Joe confessed. "All my life I've never felt that I've had much to lose, but now that I do, it's makin' me jumpy."

Joe had told Fiona all about Ellen Johnson, Dr. Taylor, and Mrs. Hamilton and her fine Virginia City mansion. "There are a lot of nice folks up on the Comstock Lode. I especially like Dr. Taylor and Dan DeQuille. And . . . well, you won't believe this . . . but I learned to read, Fiona. Now I can read and write."

She laughed. "Joe, that's wonderful! I thought I'd be the one to finally teach you, but that's fine." She winked at him and it made his heart flutter. "We'll have all kinds of other nice things to do, won't we."

Joe gulped and thought about their wedding night so fresh in his mind. He could think of plenty of things they could do that were nice and not so nice. What a night they had had together! Compared to the hurried times they'd made love while traveling with the wagon train, last night at the Roderus house was absolutely the best ever and they'd not been able to get enough of each other. In fact, they'd made love standing up and giggling right in the middle of packing to leave this morning. And it had probably shown because Faxon and his wife had been blushing as bad as themselves when they'd said good-bye.

"Come back and visit when you've had your honeymoon and need a little change of scenery," Faxon had urged. "You'll always be welcome here."

It had been a tearful farewell for Fiona and Milly. Joe knew that they couldn't come back and visit . . . ever . . . even if they wanted, because of the Peabody brothers.

But now the sun was shining and the air was scented with sage because the rain had softly fallen early this morning. Joe and Fiona had to ride their horses off to the side of the road just before they reached Virginia

City in order to let two huge freight wagons pass. They found a good spot to let their horses blow while they dismounted and stretched their legs. Rip spotted a jackrabbit and went after it with a vengeance. He overtook and caught the rabbit, then brought it back and enjoyed his usual nourishment. Rip even ate the bones, but he did spit out the hair and those long ears.

"That dog of yours is kinda scary because he's so big, fast, and vicious," Fiona said, keeping her distance from Joe's wolf-dog.

"Once he figures out that you're his friend, you'll never have a better or more loyal one," Joe replied.

Fiona returned to gazing off toward the west. From their vantage point they could look far out across Lake's Crossing to admire the silver thread that was the Truckee River. Towering above it all stood the magnificent Sierra Nevada Mountains.

"Will the mountains where you take us be as beautiful as these?" Fiona asked, her dark eyes luminous with happiness.

"They will be," he promised. "I think we'll head for the Teton Range up in Wyoming. Those peaks are not as big, but they're more jagged. They lift right out of the ground, Fiona, not like these that sorta slope up to the sky. Wait until you see the Tetons."

"I can hardly wait. But mostly, I'm yearning to see our daughter and my father."

At the mention of her father, Joe's smile faded. He supposed that he had to tell her about the death of old Brendan McCarthy. However, Joe felt he was doing no wrong when he gilded the lily just a bit and ended up saying, "Your father had stopped drinking up in Virginia City and was happy when he suddenly died of heart failure. And his last words were of *you,* Fiona. And of his granddaughter. He loved you both very much."

Fiona cried and made him promise that they could visit her father's grave, if only for a few minutes, before leaving the Comstock Lode.

"Sure," Joe said, knowing he couldn't deny his new bride this last farewell. "But first we'll get Jessica and we'll all say goodbye to your father on our way out."

Joe helped Fiona back into the saddle and they rode on into Virginia City, sticking to the back streets because neither of them wanted to be seen or recognized.

"Oh, my gawd!" Joe shouted, standing upright in his stirrups.

"What!"

"Beth Hamilton's mansion has burned to the ground!"

Joe spurred his Palouse hard and Fiona was right behind. When they reached the mansion, the ashes were cold, so it was clear that the mansion had burned a day or two before. Joe dismounted and surveyed the devastation, shaking his head in sadness and almost disbelief. The stable where Jasper, Beth's horse, had been was still standing unhurt, but the horses had been taken away.

"Is this what's left of the mansion you were staying at?" Fiona asked.

"Yeah," Joe whispered. "I hope that Beth and Ellen weren't inside when it all went up in flames."

"What could have happened?"

Joe had a bad feeling about the answer to that question. Not so long ago, he had dynamited the Shamrock Mine and burned down Ike Grady's shack. Had the Peabody brothers somehow already made the connection, and taken revenge on poor Mrs. Hamilton while hoping to catch him asleep in the night?

"Hold my reins for a minute," Joe said, handing them to Fiona and then hurrying into the barn.

Just like the Mormon Eli Purvis, Joe had chosen to hide his money in a metal box or can in the barn. And now he dug up the can and counted the money that he had left from the sale of the wagon and horses he'd taken up at Lake Tahoe along with the timber he'd sold. It came to just over four thousand dollars, and Joe figured he and Fiona had earned every penny of it.

Joe tossed the big tin can aside and handed a fistful of money to Fiona, whose eyes widened with surprise. "Joe, where did you get all this money?"

"Here and there," he said. "Put it deep in a pocket."

"But why don't you hold onto it?"

"I'm keepin' a thousand and you've got about three. It's always best to divvy it up just in case there's trouble."

Fiona tried to hand the money back to Joe, but he wouldn't hear of it, so she gave up for the time being.

"Where can we find your friends Beth and Ellen?" Fiona asked.

"I don't know," he replied, getting a real bad feeling down deep inside. "But I think we had better get Jessica back from the Catholics and leave."

"Without even knowing what happened to Beth and Ellen?" Fiona asked, clearly upset.

"We can ask about the fire and those ladies when we get down to St. Mary's to claim our Jessica. They'll know all about what happened here just in the few days I was gone."

Fiona handed Joe his reins and he vaulted into the saddle. "Fiona, I got a feeling we're runnin' out of time up here. Let's hurry, girl!"

Down the mountainside they trotted to the beautiful Catholic church. Joe and Fiona tied their horses at the gate and rushed inside to claim Jessica, but Father O'Connor intercepted them in the hallway.

"It's you!" he said, his voice hard as he confronted Fiona, and then turned his attention to Joe. "Haven't you brought enough heartache to that child already!"

"We'll get to that in a minute, Father. But first, what happened up at the Hamilton Mansion? Are Mrs. Hamilton and Mrs. Ellen Johnson all right?"

"They're fine. It was arson. Someone torched the mansion in the middle of the night. But they escaped and are staying at a hotel up on C Street."

Joe's broad shoulders sagged with relief. "I sure am glad to hear that."

"It had something to do with you, Mr. Moss. You are in great danger right now."

"Where is our Jessica?" Joe demanded. "We've come for her, Father, and we ain't leaving without our daughter."

"Your lives are in danger and you're not

336

even married!"

"We are now," Joe announced, proudly dragging yesterday's marriage certificate out of his shirt pocket. "Where is she, Father?"

The priest studied the marriage certificate with shaking hands, and then looked from one to the other before saying, "Please, for the love of God, you must understand that Jessica is happy here . . . and safe. Don't you realize the danger that child will also be in if you take her with you?"

But Fiona wasn't listening. "Father O'Connor, you swore to me that I could have her back. And now I've legally got her father's name to give to the child."

"This is just all wrong," the priest said stubbornly.

"She's ours!" Fiona cried. "And you gave me your word that you'd only keep her until I returned."

"There's blood on *both* your hands!" O'Connor shouted. "And I just can't in God's good name —"

Joe had heard enough. He knew that the priest believed he was doing what was best for Jessica, but the man was wrong. He and Fiona were going to start a new life together up in Wyoming. Far away from all the blood and trouble of their past. He would teach Jessica to swim in clear creeks, track animals, ride horses, judge the weather, and discover the beauty of nature in every leaf, flower, and blade of sweet meadow grass.

"I'll go find her," Joe said, breaking away and starting toward the church.

"No!" the priest cried. "Please, *they're watching and you've walked into their trap!*"

Joe stopped dead in his tracks. He turned around to face the priest. "Who is watching?"

Father O'Connor raised his hand and pointed to the horsemen that were suddenly surging over a hilltop not more than a half mile to the east. "I think you know who they are and why they're coming for you both. Your only chance is to get on your horses and ride. I'll try to stop them. Make them understand that mercy is. . . ."

Joe wasn't listening to the priest, and his blood froze in his veins. The riders were Peabody brothers and they had a whole lot of company. Joe quickly counted about a dozen horsemen, and every one of them had either a rifle or a pistol in his hand. There would be no talking them out of killing by the good-hearted priest or anyone else. And there would be no trial. All there would be was death for himself and his bride, Mrs. Fiona Moss.

"Fiona!" he shouted, grabbing her and

338

swinging her up onto the sorrel mare's back. "Ride!"

She was pale and shaking, but Joe didn't have time to argue. Instead, he grabbed the rifle out of his own scabbard, took aim, and fired. The first rider took a slug in the chest and flipped over backward into the brush. Joe heard the priest wailing and praying. He winged a second rider, but they kept coming, and now they were firing back.

"Ride hard, Fiona! I can't kill them all!"

"I won't have us torn apart again!"

"I'll catch up!" he bellowed, knowing that one of them was going to get killed at any moment. "I'll find you again! I *swear* it!"

Joe whacked the fast sorrel mare across the rump, and it took off at a hard run. Father O'Connor ran in front of Joe, shouting at the onrushing horsemen to stop shooting. Then, suddenly, he took a bullet in the thigh and crashed to the earth, writhing in pain with blood spurting from his wound.

"Damn you boys!" Joe shouted, taking aim on the lead rider. It was a Peabody, and Joe Moss almost smiled when he shot him in the head and watched him somersault off his racing horse.

Three down, but they were so close now Joe could see their eyes. He fired again and again, killing another Peabody and also one of their hired gunmen. That left one brother, but there wasn't time enough to pick him out from the others, and Joe knew he was about to die. Then Rip, with a deep rumble in his throat, charged the onrushing men and horses. As much as Joe's deadly fire, the sight of the huge beast sent their terrified horses swerving away from the wolfdog. And just as suddenly as it began, the charge ended as Peabody gunmen whipped their frightened horses up the grade and back toward the center of town. The riderless mounts went bucking and kicking into the brush, finally disappearing over the rocky hills.

"Rip!" Joe called, watching one of his attackers dismount and lay on the ground to take good aim at the dog. "Rip!"

Oblivious of the bullets coming his way, Rip whirled and came loping back to Joe and the fallen priest.

"Father, how bad are you hit?" Joe asked, amazed at the amount of blood the priest was rapidly losing.

"I'm all right," O'Connor managed to whisper.

But he *wasn't* all right. The bullet must have severed a vein in the man's leg, and the now priest was bleeding out right before

Joe's eyes. Joe still had that old bandanna around his neck, and now he used it to tie off the wound and staunch the flow of blood.

"Go on!" the priest begged. "Run for your life and never come back!"

"If I take the pressure off this leg, you might be dead in minutes." Joe glanced up the hill toward Virginia City. He could see that his attackers were regrouping, and knew they would soon make another, smarter charge . . . and that this time he wouldn't be able to survive. "Father, where the hell are all your nuns when you really need 'em?"

"They're shopping in Carson City."

"Shopping?"

"Yes," Father O'Connor gritted out. "The sisters may be angels on earth, but they still get hungry."

"Where is my Jessica?"

"She's with them. Safe. Safe like she's always been when she's been here with us at St. Mary's."

Joe twisted around and stared at the dust trail left by Fiona's racing mare. She was not to be seen. Thank gawd Fiona was out of danger, at least temporarily!

"Go!" O'Connor begged, looking faint

and weak. "I'm begging you for the love of God!"

Joe almost ran for his Palouse and let the priest bleed to death. But he just couldn't do it, and he turned to see that the last of the Peabody brothers was furiously exhorting his gunmen to attack once more. They had formed a line and they were about to charge back down the hill with guns blazing.

"Inside to the altar," the priest begged. "They won't dare kill you in such a sacred place."

"Sorry, Father, but you're wrong about that," Joe said. "But then again, we can't make a stand out here in the open."

He scooped up Father O'Connor and carried the man into the church, then barricaded the doors.

"Take me to the altar of Christ," the priest begged.

Joe carried him to the altar and kept his tourniquet tight over the leg wound. His efforts seemed to be working, and he thought that Father O'Connor was going to live after all. But he needed to be seen by Dr. Taylor as soon as possible.

Joe heaved a sigh and guessed he'd never live to see his daughter or Fiona again. "Father, I sure never expected to get trapped and shot to death in a place this beautiful," he said, admiring the statues of the saints, knowing he wouldn't be chosen to join them in Heaven. "I never would have guessed it."

"You're not going to die now," the priest said between his praying. "As God is my witness, you're *not* going to die here this day."

"That a promise?" Joe asked, not believing it. "Are you gonna pray all the Peabody gunmen away?"

Rip was resting in the aisle, tongue out but hackles still raised.

"I don't allow dogs in my church," the priest said. "But in this one case, I'll make an exception."

"Thank you," Joe said.

"Joe Moss, you could have saved yourself by leaving me outside. That was very brave and I know in my heart that you're a good, Christian man. I didn't think that before, but I do now. Have a little faith because Jesus and I are going to save you."

"Father, are you talking about my life . . . or my soul?"

"Both," O'Connor whispered. "I know a secret place where you and that wolf can hide here and never be found."

"Never?"

"Pick me up and we'll go there."

343

Joe picked the priest up. Now he heard pounding on the church doors. "I hope this hiding place is real close, Father."

"Very close," the priest whispered, weakly pointing toward a hallway and then finally a little door. "In here, Joe Moss. In here."

Joe and Rip rushed into a small library carrying the wounded priest. "Father, where do we go now? There's no place in here to hide."

"That Bible on the shelf. Pick it up, Joe."

"Father, I. . . ."

"Pick it up, Joe Moss!"

When Joe picked up the Bible, he was amazed, because the bookcase slowly turned to reveal a rock-lined passage, or maybe it was just a hiding hole. Joe couldn't tell.

"Put me down in that chair," O'Connor commanded. "I'll take a moment to pray and then hobble out to face them."

"And they won't kill you for hiding me?"

"They wouldn't dare!"

Joe and Rip disappeared into the priest's secret place, and when the bookshelf closed behind, they were plunged into total darkness.

"Good-bye, Joe Moss and Dog," the priest whispered. "Please go far away and *never* return."

Joe heard distant voices and then the

pounding of boots on tile. He still had his handgun, his bowie knife, and his tomahawk. Beside him in the darkness, Rip growled low, and Joe asked the big dog to be still and quiet. Rip obeyed. Now Joe crouched in the darkness, wondering if he and his dog would be found. And if they were, he hoped that he would be able to sink the blade of his tomahawk into the last Peabody left standing.

I'll do 'er if they open that bookcase, he vowed. *I'll kill as many more as I can get before they kill me so they can't hunt down my Fiona.*

But the running footfalls faded, as did the angry shouting voices after a long time. Rip began to snore softly. The bookcase never opened and Joe Moss was never found.